Outcast

Part Two
The Irish Connection

Claire Voet

First published in 2023 by Blossom Spring Publishing
Outcast The Irish Connection © 2023 Claire Voet
ISBN 978-1-7392326-8-9
E: admin@blossomspringpublishing.com
W: www.blossomspringpublishing.com

In memory of my beautiful mother,
Pamela Lorraine.

Love was, love is, love is eternal…

Prologue

Hooves thudded in the darkness, stopping at the paddock behind Aberdoch Manor. The pony gave a guttural snort, forming a cloud of breath in the cold night air. Fergus jumped down and patted the animal gratefully on its sleek neck. The moon shone platinum over Aberdoch Manor. A sizable part of it to the left had been burnt out and was nothing more than a smouldering of blackness. Fergus crept towards the entrance, alert and ready with his sword in hand, should anyone be watching and still waiting for his return. He carefully pushed the heavy wooden door open; it creaked in protest, as did the floorboards entering inside.

It was eerily quiet, the stench of smoke was overpowering, as was the spine-chilling sensation of death that hung in the air. A heavy weight of grief consumed his whole body as he rushed towards the foot of the stairs. She was still there. Still lying in her own pool of sticky, congealed blood. The Red Coats had not removed her corpse yet. He knelt down and scooped her limp, lifeless frame into his arms. "Shona, oh Shona, how could they have done this tae you?" A sob caught the back of his throat as he struggled to speak again. "I'm… I'm so sorry, sister… I should have protected ye." He held her close for a moment, his tears dripping onto her pale, cold face and blue, chapped lips. He placed her back down on the floor with care and then made his way upstairs.

Creeping slowly along the dark corridor, he was guided with nothing more than the moonlight shining in from the window downstairs and a hole in the roof above his head where the fire had ripped its way through the cladding. He gingerly pushed open the bedroom doors one by one as he passed by. Some of the rooms were badly damaged by the fire, and again, the smell of smoke caught him off guard. He entered the end room - the McDaniel Clan meeting room, with the clan emblem being the focal point of the room. He had painted it himself, and thankfully, it was unspoilt with no obvious fire damage, other than the odd dark smudge. He walked across the wooden floor with tears clouding his eyes again, staring hard at it. There was a white horse with a long, thick mane, encompassed by a design of tartan, and beneath the horse it read *Virtue – Faith – Honour – To The End*, embedded on a Scottish flag with a sword cutting through the entire image. As he turned around, he then noticed the blood smeared all over the floor, up the walls opposite the emblem and even on the velvet drapes framing the small window. There were no bodies, none in any of the rooms, which meant only one thing, the Red Coats had removed all of the dead members of Clan McDaniel, but for some reason they had not taken Shona yet, perhaps they had left her there as bait, hoping to lure Fergus and Ella back.

He dashed through to the master bedroom and collected some important belongings. He pulled open a drawer and fished out a small piece of paper. He unfolded it, squinting against the lack of light in the room, trying to read. Satisfied at last, he found what he was looking for, he then placed the paper in his sporran and went into the children's rooms next to collect a few belongings - clothes and items he thought might bring some kind of comfort.

With a shovel from the barn, he dug furiously, all his anger and grief overflowing with each harsh blow into the frosted soil. Eventually, the hole was deep enough.

He kissed her icy forehead poking out of the blanket he had wrapped her body in. "I promise with all ma heart

I'll look after yer bairns… Lilly and Ian… Dinnae fash, sister. Sleep tight, wee one." He kissed her again for the last time and then lowered her body gently into the grave.

Wild is the music of autumnal winds amongst the faded woods.

William Wordsworth

Chapter One
Dublin, Ireland 1746

Seagulls squawked, dipping in and out of a blanket of grey smothering Dublin port. Occasional tall masts managed to poke through the curling fingers of mist caressing the many vessels of different shapes and sizes. On the dock it was mayhem as usual with battles taking place, everyone clambering, reaching for their trunks and portmanteaus of personal belongings, while traders collected wooden chests stocked with produce from all around the world.

Fergus, Ella and their nephew Ian, and niece Lilly, stood on dry land at last, huddled against a wall, sheltering from passers-by. Fergus pulled out the piece of paper from inside of his brown tunic coat, reading the address out loud. "We'll need tae get tae the village of Tallaght," he said, thoughtfully, his coppery eyebrows meeting together below a mop of auburn waves.

"Is it far?" Ella glanced down at the children. They looked exhausted, not only from the journey but from grief too. No eleven and eight year old should have witnessed the brutality they had. Scenes of men they knew well, their uncle's clan members, killed so horrifically and their own mother falling to her death from the top of the stairs. Such images would likely bare deep psychological scars and haunt them for the rest of their lives. And now here they were in a foreign land, a busy city, a far cry from the countryside of Aberdoch, near Eyemouth in Scotland.

Ian held his little sister's hand tightly. She cuddled a doll she'd had since birth, its clothes and fake hair smelled of home, of Aberdoch Manor.

"We cannae walk it, we'll need a carriage," replied Fergus, folding the paper back up and placing it once more in his pocket.

The carriage pulled by two black horses made its way down the dusty narrow streets of Tallaght, passing rows of scruffy, terraced, squat houses. Locals went about their business, some chatting in doorways, others perched on a chair for comfort by the roadside catching up with the neighbours, while children played happily on the streets. There was a strong sense of a tightknit community in these parts, located west of Dublin.

The mist had not reached as far as Tallaght but the sky was still grey and heavy, threatening rain.

The horses trotted out of the village and continued down a small lane, which gave way to a clearing, revealing a large Georgian style property, shaded by a mature oak tree and surrounded by lush gardens. The carriage came to a standstill in the circular forecourt of Oakland House, known to all as Oaklands, just as a tall, broad shouldered, well dressed gentleman left the property. He stopped at the top of the steps, questioning why a carriage full of strangers should be on his land. As he approached them, recognition swept over his handsome face. "Cousin Fergus!" He rushed over to Fergus and hugged him tightly, both delighted and very surprised to see him in Dublin. After the initial hugs and happiness of seeing each other had been exchanged, Michael McDaniel glanced over at the rest of the family.

"Michael, this is Ella, ma wife." Fergus beckoned Ella to step closer.

"Yer wife? I didnae ken ye were married. Ye kept that quiet, Cousin and no for good reason... such a bonnie lass, the whole world needs tae ken!" He took Ella's hand and gently kissed it.

"It's a pleasure to meet you Mr McDaniel," Ella replied coyly, her cheeks turning a pale pink.

"Is that an English accent I detect?" He stood back, taking a better look at her.

"Yes," she replied nervously, wondering if he too had a dislike to the English as most Scots did. His smile did not falter, so it seemed not. "And are these yer bairns?" he asked looking down at Lilly and Ian with questioning eyes.

"No," said Fergus. "These are Shona's children, Lilly and Ian."

"Never!" He bent down on his haunches to take a closer look at Lilly. "Hello wee Cousin, we've never met. What a lovely dolly ye have there."

Lilly didn't respond, and with her head hung low, she held her brother's hand even tighter.

"And wee Ian, my goodness, the last time I saw you, ye were no more than a bairn in yer mother's arms."

Ian forced a small smile to be polite.

Michael stood up and faced Fergus again. In a hushed tone, he asked, "so where's Shona?

Despite his attempt at being discreet, his question was heard by all. The moment of silence that followed and solemn faces gave him his answer. "I'm so sorry, I really am," he said, holding back his own tears. He had been fond of Shona just as he was of Fergus. As children, he and his siblings had played on the grounds of Aberdoch Manor, especially through the summer months, when his own mother and father had come to stay with Fergus and Shona's parents. In his late teens his parents had moved to Ireland and since his parent's passing, he had remained in Ireland. Contact had become scarce with the rest of the family after that, only coming together for weddings and funerals.

"We've had some trouble at Aberdoch Manor," Fergus said, aware that the word *trouble* sounded like a huge understatement. "I wondered if we might stay for a short while, Michael, jist until we can…"

"Cousin, of course ye can! Clodagh will be thrilled tae have ye all stay wi' us and ye must meet our wee daughter, Mary." He patted Fergus' arm with affection.

"A smile of relief appeared on Fergus' lips, as on Ella's too."

A rumble of thunder sounded in the distance and the clouds had become even darker, giving way to a few spots of large rain drops. Fergus paid the coachman who was patiently waiting, intrigued by this family reunion.

"Come, let's get ye inside before the heavens open." Michael led the way as they followed up the steps. They were immediately greeted by Alfred, the only male servant at Oaklands, young and enthusiastic, used for heavy work and also for tending the gardens. He took their luggage and whisked it off to another part of the house for safe keeping before rushing off to find Anna the housekeeper to notify her of the guests that would be needing rooms and dinner that evening.

The McDaniels entered a large drawing room, opulently furnished with plush reds sofas, quality rugs, ornaments that were obviously of great value and many antiques that Ella suspected to be family heirlooms. She was impressed once again; it seemed the McDaniels were a wealthy family, although Aberdoch Manor was not ostentatious by any means but impressive nonetheless, as was Taig Na Mara, Aunt Ava's home on the isle of Arran. Very different from her own family and upbringing in Hampshire, living in a small cottage with an alcoholic father who raised his hands too often to her mother, herself and sister.

4

Clodagh entered the room. She wore a peach coloured gown, its tight bodice with a low-cut square neckline showed off her graceful neck. The bodice was lavishly trimmed with lace throughout giving way to a long flowing skirt covering her bump.

"Fergus McDaniel, well I never!" She rushed towards him and Fergus greeted her with a broad smile and a dutiful kiss.

"Ye havenae changed a bit, although I see ye're expecting an addition tae the family," he grinned. "Clodagh, meet ma wife, Ella."

Ella stood up, feeling slightly inferior and underdressed in Clodagh's presence, although she soon realised they actually did share something in common - they were both with child and by the size of Clodagh's stomach, Ella presumed her to be around seven months gone, two more than herself.

"Wife? And are these your bairns? I know we've not seen each other, Fergus, for a long time but…"

"They are Shona's children," Michael intercepted quickly. "I'll tell you later," he added, to save the pain of them explaining.

Clodagh dragged her quizzical eyes from her husband back to the children. "What are your names?" she asked, softly.

The children seemed uncomfortable at being put on the spot by a strange lady that they had never met, even if she was family.

"Ian and Lilly," Ella replied for them. "I'm afraid they are very tired after the journey," she smiled apologetically.

Clodagh took a moment to try and make sense of it all. So Fergus' wife was English and the children were Shona's, although Shona wasn't travelling with them, which was a mystery on its own. And why had they turned up now, in Dublin, unannounced? She displayed a reassuring smile at the children. "Hello Ian and Lilly, we're so glad... so very glad... that you're here with us in Dublin." She looked at Ella and said, "Our daughter Mary, she's six, she's with Nanny just now, I'll send for her to collect them and get them settled... cleaned up and changed," Clodagh added, noticing their grubby, dishevelled looking clothes and the dirt under their fingernails.

Ella studied Clodagh closely. She was a beautiful lady, eloquently spoken with a delicate hint of an Irish accent, obviously well bred. Lilly moved closer to Ella; her body language showed anxiety of being parted from her aunt. This didn't go unnoticed by Clodagh. She looked directly at Ella and said, "Or would you prefer to go up to their room and see to them both yourself?"

"I think that would be wise, thank you," Ella smiled, gratefully.

"Very good, let's leave the men to catch up, and I'll call Nanny to introduce you all," Clodagh said, glancing over at Fergus and Michael, knowing they had much to speak about, and she could catch up with Fergus' news later.

Hazleton Farm, Hampshire, England

Christmas Day 1945

"Merry Christmas!" Ruth called out above the chatter and clinking of cutlery, raising a glass. "And I can't tell you how happy," her voice wobbled slightly but she managed to continue nonetheless, "how happy I am to have the family all together again, safe and well!" Her eyes were watery, but she had promised herself she would not get too emotional in front of them, although it wasn't easy with it being the first Christmas after the war, and she had every right to feel emotional, and extremely grateful.

"Merry Christmas!" they all replied in unison, before digging into a feast of roast goose and all the trimmings.

Henry was uncharacteristically quiet, thinking back to the Christmases he had spent away from home. He felt undeniably blessed to be back in the bosom of his family, despite them getting on his nerves most of the time, but he was fully aware just how lucky he was - there were plenty who had not made it home, including many of his own friends. And then his thoughts drifted to Adam and his sudden arrival out of the blue. "So, Sis, why isn't your fiancé spending Christmas day with us? I thought you two would be inseparable." He grinned at Molly from across the table.

"He's with his family today. I'll see him tomorrow." Her aloof tone took most by surprise, although Henry should have known better than to tease his sister. Aunt Daphne threw him a warning glare to stop, aware of the impact Adam's arrival must have had on Molly, given the circumstances.

"Darling, I'm sure it was a shock Adam turning up like that after missing for so long, but surely you are thrilled, aren't you?" Ruth asked, warily. Molly didn't seem to be as pleased as they all thought she would be, especially given how she had been pining for him for so long, desperate to know if he was alive or dead.

"I thought you'd be really excited," said Emily, popping a roast potato into her mouth, confused as her mother was by Molly's glum expression.

"Don't you love him no more?" Charlie asked. The baby of the family at twelve years old was beginning to realise that girls were tricky and love seemed complicated, something he'd rather steer clear of for as long as possible.

"If you ask me, there's something not right about the lad," George said, sitting at the head of the table. As any father would be, he was protective and he had his doubts about Adam's story. It just didn't sit well with him.

"Can you all please just stop!" Molly said, raising her voice.

Silence followed as they continued eating, until Ruth decided to rescue the happy Christmas she had been dreaming of. "How's the preparations going Auntie, with the opening of the hotel?"

"I think we are on track after a difficult start but…"

The conversation flowed once more, as did the wine, and everyone began to relax; everyone apart from Molly, who couldn't wait to get away and be alone with her thoughts. And as soon as she had the opportunity, after helping clean up the kitchen, she slipped out of the back door and walked through the farm yard, perching down on a stone wall outside of the piggery. The moon was partially cloaked by a wispy cloud. The air was icy and she shivered, despite having grabbed her coat on the way out. Benji had followed her outside and waddled up to her, pushing his wet nose into her hand. She stroked him with affection, and unable to hold it all in any longer, she broke down and cried, sobbing into the old sheepdog's warm and comforting fur. She then looked up at the sound of footsteps approaching. Emily reached Molly's side and perched herself down on the wall. "Brrr! Bit nippy out here," she said, bumping shoulders affectionately with her older sister by only eighteen months. Molly didn't reply.

"What is it, Moll? You know you can tell me anything."

Molly sighed heavily. "I grieved a long time for him, Emily, a long time and just when I started to move on, he came back from the dead."

"I know it's a shock, but it means you can be happy again. He's alive and he's well, albeit looking a little different after operations to his face, but still." She fell pensive for a moment and then said, "I have to say they did a fantastic job of fixing him up. Apart from the small scar under his chin, you wouldn't know, unless you knew him before."

"That's just it," said Molly looking directly at Emily. "I wonder if I really did know him before, I feel that my memory serves me poorly. His eyes seem darker than I recall and his voice deeper, and now his surgery to his face… he's not the man I fell in love with."

"It's not all about looks though, Molly. I mean, you love him, he loves you, you are engaged to be married. He's still the same person inside."

"No he's not. How could he ever be the same person after what he's been through?" Molly cried, wiping her tears with her cold palms. Benji snuggled up closer to her, sensing how upset she was and she gave him a grateful stroke around his ears.

"I know. It's going to be hard for many men returning home after what they saw, what they had to do. I can't begin to imagine how…"

"Emily, I've not told you everything," Molly confessed.

"Go on." Emily reached out and touched her hand, curious to know more.

"I'm in love with someone else. Ross McDaniel." There, she had said it. In fact, she had planned to tell the whole family yesterday when she had arrived, but with Adam suddenly turning up out of the blue like he had, her good news had fallen by the wayside.

The name Ross McDaniel rang a bell and then Emily realised why. "The gardener from Aberdoch Manor, who called you yesterday evening?" It all started to fall into place now. She had wondered why the gardener needed to speak to Molly on Christmas Eve and why he should bother her while she was on holiday at home with her family, having only left Scotland that same morning.

"I lied to you, yesterday. When he called, I said it was about Aberdoch Manor, but it wasn't… he wanted to wish me a merry Christmas and tell me that he missed me and couldn't wait for my return."

"Wow!" Emily looked taken aback. "And I thought it was me that always had the complicated love life. Moll, what are you going to do?"

"I don't know, Emily, I really don't," she sighed feeling hopeless. "I don't want to hurt Ross, I can't…"

"Alright, so tell me what's so special about this Ross McDaniel?"

Molly looked back at her sister, not really knowing how to answer her question, it was more loaded than Emily was aware of. "When he kisses me, its magical." She smiled dreamily, but then her face soon clouded remembering also how much he reminded her of Fergus. How could she possibly tell Emily what happened at Aberdoch? That after touching an ancient yew tree, nicknamed the Ghost Tree, she suddenly had the ability to see her own past life and the man she had once been married to happened to be Ross' ancestor? Even thinking about it sounded in her mind to be far too outrageous for anyone to comprehend. Henry had handled it amazingly well and it was probably only because of his creative writer's mind that he was able to digest such a bizarre story. But Aunt Daphne had not been so understanding and was worried that Molly would end up like poor old Uncle Larry who had resided in a mental institution. Vicar Norman and his wife Joan thought pretty much the same as Aunt Daphne did, and even Ross himself struggled with the notion of a possible past life connecting Molly with his ancestor.

"It's always magical in the beginning, Molly. Every romance starts like that. You just need to get the magic back with Adam."

"So, so you think I should end it with Ross?" A tear trickled down the side of her nose. The idea of finishing with Ross was too painful to consider right now.

"It's not my decision to make. But you had something special with Adam once, enough for you to accept his proposal of marriage, enough for you to miss him like mad for so long."

Molly jumped down from the wall. "It's getting too cold, let's go back inside," she said, thinking about Emily's words. Yes, she had accepted Adam's proposal, she had been so excited, so incredibly in love with him then. Now she felt nothing but terribly confused. "You won't say anything to anyone will you?" She faced Emily with pleading eyes.

"Of course not. Spend these days, as much as you can,

getting to know Adam again, and at the end of your stay, I'm sure it will be clear." She linked arms with Molly and they walked back across the yard with Benji in tow, relieved also to be getting out of the cold as he wagged his tail.

The morning sun poked through a mound of grey clouds as Molly walked over to the goat pen wearing an old pair of dungarees and holding a tin bucket in her hand, having promised her little brother, Charlie, she would do his job of milking them for the next few days to give him a well-earned break. It was her job before she moved to Scotland, as Charlie so rightly pointed out often enough, peeved that he was now head goat milker at Hazleton Farm, a job he despised!

Inside the farmhouse, the high pitched ring of the phone echoed throughout the house as Ruth dashed to answer it. After realising the call was for Molly, she placed a hand over the receiver and shouted up the stairs and then towards the living room, if anyone knew where Molly was. Henry, with his dark, curly hair up on end, still in his pyjamas, having just pulled himself out of bed, appeared at the top of the stairs and shouted back in reply. "I heard her telling Charlie last night she's going to milk the goats for him this morning - buggered if I know why, I certainly wouldn't!" He yawned and then padded back to his room in search of a dressing gown and slippers. Now he was awake, he might as well get up.

"I'm sorry, she's busy just now, can I take a message?" Ruth asked, putting on her well-spoken telephone voice that all the Hazletons found to be most amusing. Henry in particular was able to mimic her to perfection. "Of course, I shall pass on your message. Thank you, Mr McDaniel," she replied to the voice down the line before hanging up. She frowned and walked off towards the kitchen. She found Aunt Daphne tucking into a breakfast of eggs on toast. "Auntie, who is this Ross McDaniel? It's the second time he's called now for Molly."

"He's the gardener," Daphne replied, picking up the tea pot and pouring herself another cup of tea.

"And what does he want with Molly?" Ruth asked, looking perplexed.

"It's not my place to say." She brought the tea cup to her lips and took a sip.

"Auntie, she's my daughter, surely I have a right to know."

Daphne pursed her lips. "Very well," she sighed. Ruth would find out sooner or later, so she might as well tell her. "She's been courting him. I told her to wait. I said, Molly, you should give yourself more time before stepping out with him, but she was convinced Adam was dead and never coming back."

"Oh, I see." Ruth sat down and poured herself a cup of tea. "Goodness," she said, thinking out loud, "and now Adam is back." Molly's behaviour was starting to make sense. "And is she very keen on this Ross McDaniel?"

"Keen?" Daphne gave a small humourless chuckle. "They've been practically joined at the hip for the past few weeks. I'm surprised he didn't come with us yesterday."

"Good job he didn't," Ruth said thinking about Adam. "And is he a nice lad? I mean you employed him, so he must be nice enough?"

"He's alright. I had to have words with him, filling her head with nonsense about some blessed tree that gives powers to see past lives, apparently." She omitted to tell her that Molly had ended up in hospital with hypothermia after falling into a hypnotic state at the tree while sitting in the snow. Ruth would not let Molly go back to

Scotland if she knew that.

"What?" Ruth replied incredulously.

Daphne rolled her eyes. "The Scots are a funny lot, full of superstitions and traditions."

"Sounds rather odd to me." Ruth stared back at Daphne with worried eyes.

"He means well. After my having words with him, the matter seems to have been put to rest."

"Right." Ruth sat back in her chair, unsure of what to think of Molly's new love.

Ella felt more relaxed now that the children were fed, cleaned and in bed asleep. She, too, had freshened up and changed for dinner, wearing something more suitable from the limited selection of clothes she had with her, the only clothes that Fergus had managed to retrieve from Aberdoch Manor the night before they fled Scotland. She chatted to Clodagh with ease about a number of topics, including motherhood and her knowledge of herbal medicine.

"So, tell me about the paper mill," Fergus said, taking a sip of wine, also feeling a lot more relaxed, thanks to Michael's reassurance that he would help in any way he could, and that they could stay for as long as they wished.

"I own the second paper mill in Dublin. The first belongs tae Thomas Slater, a former publisher. Three years ago I thought it was time tae give Slater a run for his money." He grinned. "And since then, another has arrived but it's far enough away. The market is proving strong enough tae sustain more than one mill in Dublin. In fact, the Royal Dublin Society are offering premiums for collection of rags to supply to us. I read they have gathered five hundred pounds worth of rags so far. I'm run ragged with supplies," he laughed. Fergus appreciated the pun with a chuckle.

"Why does a paper mill need rags?" Ella asked in her naivety, picking up on the conversation during a brief interlude from her own with Clodagh.

"Rags are used to make paper. The linen is put in a circular vat where they are beaten or ground into a watery pulp, which then allows us tae make it into paper," Michael replied, matter-of-factly.

"Interesting," Ella said, before resuming conversation again with Clodagh about the best remedy for backache during the final trimester of pregnancy.

"Maybe I could help in some way?" Fergus asked pensively.

"Why would ye want tae work at the mill?" Michael asked, bringing a glass of wine to his lips.

The maid was now clearing the table and Ella thanked her for a delicious meal.

"I'm no afraid of hard work," Fergus replied. "So, if ye need help, which it sounds tae me like ye do, what wi' ye being run ragged," he smirked. "I'm happy tae be of service."

"I could do with an extra pair of hands with the rag supplies, I suppose. It would mean negotiating the best deals ye can, keeping our profit margins as wide as possible."

"Oh I'm no stranger tae negotiation," Fergus smiled wryly.

Clodagh stood up, rubbing her back. "Shall we leave them to it and retire somewhere more comfortable?"

Ella nodded, sympathetic to Clodagh's discomfort. "Gentlemen," she smiled courteously as they both left the room.

Michael poured himself and Fergus a glass of whisky from the decanter in the centre of the table. He handed a glass to Fergus. "Fergus, I'll help ye with money, I'll no take advantage, you'll be paid a proper wage, but tell me what are yer long term plans? Dublin is a fine place tae settle with a family."

Fergus hesitated, contemplating his reply. Michael had been good enough to offer him and Ella hospitality and now a job, he deserved to know the truth. He had already told him how Shona had died, about the McKenzies and how they had attacked his own clan and the result had ended in a brutal massacre at Aberdoch Manor, but he had not told him about Ella. "I dinnae ken if we can stay in Dublin, it's no far enough away from Scotland," he replied and then took a swig of whisky.

"I really dinnae think ye need tae fash about the McKenzies any longer. They have no idea ye're here in Dublin and even if they did, would they really bother tae travel here? They killed yer men, they drove ye out of yer home - in their eyes they have won and that should be good enough."

Fergus bit his bottom lip in thought. "I'm no scared of the McKenzies," he said with conviction. "I dinnae want tae put Ella and the children at risk, and under any other circumstances I would have laid low somewhere safe in Scotland, and when the dust settled, I'd return and I'd return with men. I'd kill every last one of those bastards." His eyes gleamed with hatred for what they had done. "If I ever see one of them again, they will regret the day they were born. I will kill them with ma bare hands - after torturing them first of course, until they snivelled and begged for mercy for which there would be no mercy, not ever," he hissed.

Michael reached out to Fergus and patted his shoulder. "Of course there could be no mercy, they deserve tae suffer, aye, of course they do. But what do ye mean about you wouldnae have left under any other circumstances, what made ye leave?"

Fergus signed heavily. "Michael, what I'm about tae tell ye, please promise me ye'll keep it tae yerself, no breathe a word, no even tae Clodagh? And I ask ye no tae judge Ella either."

"Of course." He raised an eyebrow with surprise, unable to imagine what Ella could have possibly done that she should be judged.

"When I met her, I was with the Jacobite, we were fighting the Hanoverians on the outskirts of Carlisle. After the battle I spotted her running through the woods. She was being chased by three armed men."

Michael sat forward in earnest. "Why?"

"She's a healer and her healing was mistook for practising witchcraft."

"That's insane."

"Aye, of course it is but they wanted tae bring her tae trial. Anyway, while protecting her against those men, who we believed tae be working for the King, I killed two of them. I had no choice, it was tae keep her safe."

Michael nodded, picturing the scene. He himself would have done the same to keep Clodagh safe.

"When we returned tae Aberdoch, shortly after, the Red Coats came calling. They were hunting Ella, not only for witchcraft but for two counts of murder." Fergus' eyes were fixed on Michael's hoping for his understanding.

"Murder? How did they even think Ella capable of murdering two men? She's a wee slip of a lass."

"Aye, I agree, but rumour has it she killed them using witchcraft."

Michael slammed his hand down on the table. "That's outrageous!"

"They've been on our trail ever since. They even turned up at Aberdoch on the eve of the attack. We fled and have managed tae escape them so far, but I have a feeling they will no give up easily, especially should they get wind of us being in Dublin."

"But there must be a way tae sort this, tae get her pardoned?" Michael said. He topped up their glasses with more whisky. If there was one thing that made him angry it was injustice and people being wrongly accused. Everyone deserved a chance to explain themselves.

"Maybe, possibly, but at a high risk. If we cannae get her pardoned she'll hang and I'm no prepared tae lose ma wife and unborn child. What wi' the McKenzies, and Shona now gone, I think the best thing tae do is head for the Americas, far away from the British Red Coats, away from all the trouble. I need a safe place tae raise Lilly and Ian and ma own bairn when it arrives, and tae look after ma family properly, without being on the run.

Chapter Two

"Hello, Adam!" Henry opened the front door on his way to the kitchen to grab a cup of tea. He was on a well-earned tea break, having finally just finished the novel he had been writing before he got roped into Molly's research and an unexpected trip up to Aberdoch Manor with his findings. Tomorrow he would post it off to the publishers, and while waiting for their response, he would start work on a new one based loosely on the facts of Molly's personal story relating to a possible past life. Of course, a Henry Hazleton novel would never be complete without some saucy love affair or scandal, thrown in for good measure. "Can't believe you're back from the dead!" He grinned and then suddenly it came to him like a bolt of lightning - the perfect plot for one of his new characters. "Oh my God, it's staring me right in the face – back from the dead - I could kiss you, Adam Buxton!"

"Please don't!" Adam stepped back from him, warily. Molly's brother was weird and then it dawned on him that perhaps Henry preferred men. He made a mental note to avoid being alone with him. Better to be safe than sorry.

"Molls!" Henry called out from the bottom of the stairs. "Dead lover boy is here to see you!"

Molly appeared at the top of the stairs.

"I'm guessing you know which one I mean," he smirked, heading off to the kitchen.

Molly rolled her eyes and made her way downstairs. She noticed Adam's perturbed look as she came towards him.

"What did he mean by – *you know which one I mean?*"

"Take no notice, you know what he's like," she replied, not wanting to get into complicated explanations.

Adam nodded. "I'd forgotten… and I'd forgotten just how pretty you are too." He gave an appreciative whistle, admiring her trim figure in a tight pair of beige trousers. She wore her hair tied back. He preferred it down, but she still looked gorgeous. "What do you want to do today? It's entirely up to you."

She could hear the voices of her mother and Aunt Daphne somewhere nearby. "Go out for a walk," she said, grabbing her coat from the stand behind the front door, wishing to make a swift exit before they interfered. Like Emily said, she needed to spend time alone with Adam, and that meant away from prying ears and eyes. She closed the front door behind them and he opened the small white picket fence gate for her. A large goose waddled in front of them as they waited for it to pass, while somewhere in the distance a cockerel crowed. Despite it being cold, the sun was shining, although not strong enough to make a difference, but the sky was a rare incredible bright blue.

"Nice day for a walk," Adam said, reaching out and taking her hand into his own. She quickly let go of it and buttoned her coat. Somehow just touching him felt like a betrayal to Ross, yet it should have been the other way around. Adam was her fiancé and she needed to keep reminding herself of that fact. "Shall we go to our favourite place?" She smiled, digging her hands into her pockets to avoid any chance of him trying to hold her hand again.

"Favourite place? Yes of course."

She could tell from the concerned expression that he

had forgotten where their favourite place was. "You don't remember do you?"

He shook his head. "Sorry. Oh it's so annoying not remembering things."

"Our favourite place is at the lake, just before the village," she carried a hint of disappointment in her tone.

"Of course," he said, slapping his forehead, feeling such a fool. He should have known that.

"Was it a head injury that caused you to lose your memory?" They had left the estate now and were heading down a small country lane.

"They said that trauma can make you block things out. It's the mind's defence mechanism to stop you reliving and feeling the pain again."

Molly looked confused. "But memories of home surely aren't painful?"

"No, of course not, but it doesn't seem to differentiate. Some things I remember and others I don't. Molly, are you really happy I'm home?" He stopped suddenly, facing her, his eyes surveying hers closely.

"Of course I am." She managed a small smile. But he was no fool and she could see by the look in his eyes, he wasn't convinced. "Adam, I went through hell waiting for you, thinking you were dead. There was no news, nothing but silence surrounding you, even after the war had ended. You still haven't told me why you didn't come back after the war. You just said you were in France. When I pushed you to tell me more on Christmas Eve you walked away from me. For all I know, you could have been shacked up with some French tart in her boudoir all this time." She realised she had painted a scene that wouldn't have been out of place in one of Henry's novels. Adam had always been loyal to her but war changed people, changed relationships – couples were parted for months and years on end, anything could have happened.

"How could you say that?" There was hurt in his eyes. He continued to walk on.

She stood for a second, gathering her thoughts. "I'm sorry," she called out, running after him.

"It's painful to talk about," he said, giving her a sideways glance.

"I know. I'm sorry. I just want to try and understand where you've been, what you've been through. To help support you better... if I just knew, it would help."

They reached a small wooden gate and Adam pushed it open for them to walk into a field. A few grazing sheep looked up with curiosity and then continued their munching. "I'm guessing it is this way," he said, looking back over his shoulder at her.

"Yes, it's not far from here."

"I couldn't come back, because..." he paused trying to find his words, fighting his tears. "Because I didn't know who I was any more."

"Are you speaking metaphorically or literally?" Molly asked, very much aware of his memory loss.

"Both," he replied solemnly. "When he found me in a ditch on the battlefield, at first glance he thought I was dead. I lay with a heap of dead bodies surrounding me." Adam wiped a stray tear away from his cheek. Molly looked at him mournfully. "Who found you?"

"A French farmer. He risked his life pulling me out of a ditch and dragging me away to safety."

"And then what happened?"

"I don't remember him saving me and I don't remember how I got to his house, but I woke up days later in his cellar. The village doctor was there - he had seen me through the worst."

"Why didn't they take you to the hospital?"

"It was too far away and too dangerous for me to

travel. They feared the journey would have killed me, not to mention the risk of getting caught by the Jerries on the streets."

They reached the lake and stopped in front of it, both lost in their own thoughts watching the sun sparkle on the surface of the water like tiny crystals.

"Why didn't you come home when the war ended?" Molly turned to face him, still waiting for his answer.

"I didn't know who I was, let alone where home was. My belongings had been stripped from me by the Jerries when they thought I was dead."

"How did you manage to play dead, surely they must have seen you were breathing?" She was desperately trying to make sense of his story but something felt amiss, although she couldn't be sure what it was exactly; the French farmer risking his life for a British solider he didn't know or the Germans believing him to be dead.

"I was unconscious, covered in blood and bodies all around me, I suppose they presumed I was dead." His tone was bitter, feeling irritated at her questioning.

"So you just stayed with the French farmer all this time?" she continued, regardless.

"Yes, him and his wife and two young daughters. They were age seven and ten," he added quickly for reassurance, before any accusations could be thrown his way, especially as she'd thought him to be shacked up with a French tart. "Then one day, I was chopping wood and suddenly I received my first flash of memory - of home, my parents, Graham, my brother and then you."

"How is Graham?" With everything that had gone on, she had forgotten to enquire.

"He lost his right arm," he said, looking forlorn.

"I'm so sorry. I should have gone to visit your family. When the war ended, everyone was celebrating and I fell into a depression. It was like a big black cloud hanging

23

over me and it took all my strength to get out of bed and help on the farm. I think deep down inside I thought seeing them would make the loss worse. Then Aunt Daphne came to stay and offered me a fresh start in Scotland." She gave a watery smile. "I could go with you to visit Graham, and your parents, tomorrow or sometime later this week, if you like. It would be good to see your family again."

"No!" he replied, a bit too quickly, taking her by surprise. "They're away, in Cornwall visiting my sick aunt."

"So you were on your own for Christmas?"

"No, they left this morning."

"Oh, I see."

Their attention was momentarily diverted by a couple of frolicking ducks splashing around.

"What happens now, Molly?" He looked at her with so much sadness in his eyes. The thought of her turning her back on him hurt more than he could bear.

"I… I don't know, Adam. I need some time to adjust and for this all to sink in. You being here, us together again… it's all such a shock."

It had occurred to him on more than one occasion that she may have moved on and it pained him to ask, but he did anyway. "Is there someone else?"

"What? No!" Her reply had left her lips before she'd had time to consider her answer. Although it was probably for the best, she didn't want to hurt him if she wasn't sure herself yet. How she felt about Ross didn't come into the equation. It was Adam she was engaged to, committed to, not Ross, despite her wishing otherwise.

"Good, because I couldn't bear it if you were with somebody else."

"I'd be within my rights, considering I thought you were dead," she replied harshly. Her face then softened, pointing over at a bench. "Let's sit down."

"Do you remember the last time we sat here?" she said, watching a swan heave itself out of the water and wander along the muddy bank.

"You'll have to remind me, I'm afraid."

"You'd been on leave only for two days and you were due back the next morning. I cried in your arms, desperate for you not to go back, not knowing if I would ever see you again. We kissed and you told me you loved me." She turned and looked him in the eyes. "You said I'll be back, you'll see. I said don't make promises you can't keep."

"But I did keep my promise. I'm here, aren't I?" He raised his dark eyebrows as if proving a point.

"Yes, now you are. I came here day after day since receiving the telegram saying you were missing. Sitting here, the last place we had been together, made me feel close to you."

He held her tearful stare. "Molly, I love you. I love you so much." He leaned in closer and without warning, their lips met instinctively.

She looked awkwardly at him, a little breathless and still surprised by what had just happened. "Adam I… I… have to tell you something."

"Go on." He held her hand. "Whatever it is, tell me, it's fine."

She looked at him, her eyes unwavering but as much as she wanted to, it wasn't the right time. It probably never would be the right time to tell him about Ross, but sooner or later she knew she would have to, just not today.

"Molly, what is it?" he pressed, feeling anxious now.

"I'm not going to stay living here in Hampshire," she said at last. Perhaps it might put him off and he would finish with her, now he knew she wasn't staying, although she wasn't sure if she wanted him to. She wasn't sure how she felt other than utterly confused. "Aunt Daphne has been good to me; she needs my help and she has also left the hotel to me in her will. How could I possibly walk away from that?"

His eyes lit up. "Oh no you can't, you mustn't walk away and especially not because of me, I wouldn't hear of it. Molly that's wonderful news, what a future - to have your own hotel one day."

"So you won't try and stop me?" she asked hesitantly, trying to fathom what he was thinking.

"Of course not. I'll come with you," he beamed, excited at the idea of starting a new life in Scotland. In fact, it was more appealing than Molly would ever know. The further away from Hampshire, the better.

"But what will you do in Scotland?" This was far from the reaction she had expected.

"Same as what I would do here, look for a carpentry job. I'm a skilled craftsman, something'll turn up."

"I suppose Auntie was looking at converting the outbuildings into stables to offer pony trekking to the guests. It's not exactly carpentry work, more like labour, but…"

"I can do it and there will be carpentry work involved too." He was still grinning from ear to ear. "Molly, this is the fresh start we need, you and me together in Scotland!"

"But I must speak to Auntie and I need some time to think this through."

He looked at her confused. "Think what through?"

"Us, being together again. We've been apart for so long."

"I see." Disappointment grew in his eyes, and she suddenly felt guilty. She had got his hopes up and she should never have done that. She stood up and looked at him. "I'll give you my answer on New Year's Eve. It'll give me time to think and to speak to Auntie. We leave for Scotland on the second of January."

He nodded in agreement, knowing he had no choice but to wait for her answer. If he pushed her, he ran the risk of losing her. If she said no on New Year's Eve, at least he still had the next day to try and talk her round. "Very well." He stood up too, putting on a brave face. "I know it's a lot to take on, with my memory problem. You need time to think and I respect that." He managed a small smile. "As we are near the village, there must be a pub, so how about we have some lunch, my treat?"

She smiled at him. "That sounds lovely," she replied, feeling a little more at ease, now that she had more time to think.

"I wonder how Molly's getting on with Adam?" Ruth said, thinking out loud.

"Love's young dream, mmm, I wonder." Daphne filled in the last letter of the crossword puzzle in the back of the newspaper, feeling pleased with herself as she took off her glasses and popped them back into the case.

"Auntie, if she does decide to give it a go with Adam, what will happen if she doesn't go back to Scotland with you? Do you have someone to help you up there? I can always send Henry to help, Emily wouldn't leave her friends and Charlie's too young."

"Henry!" Daphne let out one of her infamous hoots. "He'd put me in an early grave, that boy and what with the click clack of that blessed typewriter, guaranteed to bring on one of my heads, no thank you very much, I shan't be needing Henry's services." She put down the newspaper on the coffee table in front of her. "There'll be no cause for concern, Molly will be coming back with me," she said with certainty.

"And how do you know that?" Ruth raised a quizzical eyebrow.

"We had a chat this morning and she said she was going back, no matter what. Besides, she'd be a fool to walk away from her inheritance over some chap, especially one she's not sure about anymore."

"Inheritance, what inheritance?" Ruth asked with surprise.

"The hotel. I thought she would have told you. There'll not be much money in the pot after I've finished doing it up, but don't worry, you'll get any little savings I have, but the hotel will go to Molly."

"Thanks," Ruth smiled sardonically.

"What's this?" George wandered into the living room.

"Auntie's going to leave the hotel to Molly, apparently."

"Oh, right." He looked at Daphne belligerently. "Molly does have siblings you know. Do you really think it fair, favouring one over the others?"

"The others are not helping me turn a rundown mansion into a hotel or will be working in it either. She deserves to reap the fruits of her labour."

"Only because you selected her, she was your chosen one," he said, flopping down in the armchair opposite.

"Now let's get one thing straight here," Daphne said, annoyed that he of all people should be telling her what to do with her money. "I saved that poor girl from going to ruin. She was in a mess, devastated over losing her fiancé and what did you two do about it? I'll tell you what - nothing."

"Auntie, that's not true. We offered all the support we could."

"By getting her to milk the goats, feed the pigs, muck out the stables, fine support that was." Her anger was more focused on George, fully aware how he bullied the children into doing chores around the farm.

"They all have their responsibilities," George said indignantly.

"Henry, Emily and Charlie won't be left out. I have some money put aside for them, in a trust, I'm not as heartless as you think," Daphne said.

"Oh really," George scoffed.

"Not that it's any of your business, George Hazleton, what I do with my money."

"You're right, I'm sorry, Auntie. George is sorry as well, aren't you George? We shouldn't have criticised your decision, after all it is your money.

George shook his head at Ruth. "Since when has it been a crime to speak one's mind?" He pointed at Daphne. "I'm not frightened of her like you are, I'm not walking around on eggshells in my own home, so as not to upset her."

"No, you go stomping around and wading in with your big size nines!" Ruth replied sharply.

"You got that right," Daphne smirked.

"Anyway, New Year's Eve," Ruth said, changing the subject, "I think we should all go to the party at the village hall, it'll be fun."

Daphne harrumphed. "Oh you can count me out."

"In that case you can count me in," George replied, making his point clear.

"Auntie, why don't you want to come?" Ruth asked with concern. She felt mean leaving her behind while they all went out and had a good time.

"I'd sooner be in bed with a good book. When you get to my age you can't be bothered making a fuss about a new year that you may not even reach the end of."

"We can live in hope," George muttered, rising to his feet. "I'm starving, what's there to eat?"

"There's some homemade vegetable soup on the stove

and you can have it with some of that loaf left over from yesterday.

"Look! Aunt Clodagh made a new dress for Isobel." Lilly held the doll up for Ella to see.

"And Mammy made one for my dolly too!" little Mary said, not wanting to be left out. She looked like her mother, with the same dark curls and deep hazel eyes.

"Oh, how beautiful!" Ella smiled at both the girls; she was glad to see Lilly much happier. It had been three weeks since they'd arrived in Dublin. Lilly had taken just over a week to come out of her shell and play with Mary. She was good with younger children, Ella noted, realising how handy that would be when the baby came along. Ian had also become more confident, helping his Uncle Fergus and Cousin Michael at the paper mill. He was gone for most of the day and they kept him occupied with organising and cutting the rags. He seemed to be enjoying it. It was a different way of life than he'd been used to, away from working on the land and looking after the ponies at Aberdoch Manor.

"I said I'd teach the girls how to make tapestries," Clodagh said, sitting in her favourite, most comfortable chair close to the fire. "If I can see over my stomach being the size of a whale, that is," she chuckled.

"You are not that big," Ella smiled sympathetically. "If I'm your size in two months from now, I'll be happy."

"Oh would you now? I'll hold you to that," Clodagh grinned. "Does that mean you'll be staying so I can compare your size?"

Ella gave a wistful sigh. "I wish." If only they could stay. She had not felt this relaxed since staying with Aunt Ava on the Isle of Arran. But Fergus was right, it would be risky to stay too long in Dublin, especially with it being easily accessible from Scotland.

"If you wish so, then why not stay?"

"It's not that simple, besides, you'll be wanting your home back soon."

"Says who? We love having you here, don't we Mary?" Mary looked up from playing with Lilly, they were having a pretend tea party with the dollies, all spread out over a dark red carpet.

"Yes," Mary replied with an enthusiastic nod.

"I would like to stay, Auntie," Lilly added sincerely.

"There you go, seems your wish has come true," Clodagh smiled.

"I feel like I should be doing something. I'm not used to so much relaxation." Ella stood up and stretched her back, feeling stiff from sitting for too long. She wasn't accustomed to Clodagh's way of life. It was a far cry from the life she once had on the road with the Jacobite when she had first met Fergus - fixing injured men, witnessing brutal injuries and death after their battles with the Hanoverians. And before that she had practised her healing skills in her home village amongst the locals, who would call upon her for aid against their various ailments. Until it all ended abruptly and she was driven away by the priest and the king's men, believing she was a witch, using witchcraft to heal. This misunderstanding had forced her to flee her home, her family and friends, but it did not stop her from healing others, nothing would do that. Healing was her calling, she just needed to find a way how to do it again, how to be useful to others in a way that made a difference.

"Enjoy the peace while you can," Clodagh said,

continuing with her tapestry.

The moonlight shone through a crack in the curtains. Lilly peered over at her brother in the next bed. They could have had their own rooms, there were plenty of them at Oaklands but they shared due to Lilly's fear of being alone since witnessing such harrowing atrocities at Aberdoch Manor. She felt safer with her big brother close. "Ian, are you awake?" She whispered loudly into the darkness.

"I am now," he groaned, rolling on his side to face her. "I cannae sleep again."

He yawned. "You should work at the mill, if only you were a boy. That'll make ye sleep."

"Do ye like working there? What's it like?"

"Busy, noisy, but everyone is friendly and it's interesting tae think that from a piece of rag, paper is made. Aye, I do like working there. I quite fancy maself as a paper miller one day." He smiled, imagining himself managing a big workforce, just like Cousin Michael did. "Lilly, if you give me that doll ye always walk around with, I can make it into paper for you!" he teased.

"No! You are never going tae take Isobel. She's mine, since I was a bairn." Her thoughts drifted back to home again, to her mother. "I miss Mammy... I miss her so much that it hurts right here." She pointed to her heart, with tears in her eyes.

"I do, too. But if you close yer eyes, ye can see her whenever ye want to."

"How?"

"Imagine her baking, or saying goodnight tae you... anything ye want."

Lilly closed her eyes and concentrated. She could see her mother baking bread and herself sitting at the large wooden table watching her. She yawned, continuing with her fond memories of home, reliving them like they had happened that same day, and a moment later she had fallen asleep.

Ian checked on her, noticing it had gone quiet. The silver glow of the moon caught the left side of her face, emphasising her long lashes and little button nose. Realising his sister was asleep, he sighed contentedly and closed his eyes.

Fergus slipped into bed next to Ella. She was reading by the aid of a soft candlelight on the bedside table. He glided a hand over her protruding tummy. "Is it a suitable bedtime story for this wee one?"

She chuckled. "Maybe when she, or he, becomes of age to appreciate romance."

"Romance, ha? I'm no romantic enough for ye that ye must read about it in books?"

"You are very romantic, Laird McDaniel, as a rule, but I hardly see you these days, what with you being at the mill all day long… I fear I will forget what romance feels like soon if I don't read about it."

"Ella, ye ken I'm only doing this tae raise more money tae leave… although if I'm honest, it's no hardship working at a papermill."

"I've been thinking," she said, snapping the book shut. The candle flickered erratically from the sudden draught of the book closing, and then stabilised its glow once more.

"Thinking, oh aye, sounds dangerous," he teased.

She smacked his arm playfully. "If we were to move into the countryside, away from the centre of Dublin, could we stay here, in Ireland? I'm certain Ian and Lilly would like it; it'll be more like Aberdoch."

"And what are we supposed tae do in the countryside? What would we live from in the long term?"

"With the savings we have and the money you're earning at the paper mill, we could start a farm, instead of using it to travel and start a new life in America."

"Farm? I dinnae ken much about farming, Ella."

"You could learn… we could learn. At least we would all have something to do, including the children."

"Something to do?" he echoed.

Ella wriggled back into the large duck feathered pillows. "I'm really grateful for the hospitality Clodagh and Michael have given us, I really am, but this is not my way of life, it's not our way of life. I have nothing to do here. I can't bake because they have Mrs O'Connor, the cook, to do that. I can't garden because they have a gardener. I can't clean because they have a maid. Even the nanny wants to take Lilly from me and I have to stop her sometimes, I'm not used to this pampered way of life… I feel redundant."

"Ella, it's only temporary and ye are with child now. Why don't ye ask Mrs O'Connor if ye can do so some baking, if ye're that bored. I'm sure she'll no mind."

"I already tried. I suggested yesterday that I make a cake and she looked horrified, as if I had just suggested I cut off one of her limbs."

Fergus' shoulders shook under the covers from laughter.

"Fergus, how long would it take for you to raise the money to start a farm?"

"It's no a question of how much money I can raise, I'd enough now, but it's best tae have plenty put aside for any eventuality, for emergencies so tae speak. Ma concern is if the Red Coats come looking for us, we'd…"

"You mean come looking for me. It's me they are seeking, not you. But why would they? How would they even know I am here in Ireland?"

"Aye, Michael said the same," Fergus sighed. "But

with the English governing Ireland, there could be communication between the Red Coats here and in England although a slim chance, I ken that."

"And the only alternative to staying is that we leave for America, a long crossing to the other side of the world? I'm not sure it wise to put the children through that, Fergus, after everything that's happened."

"Aye, I understand what ye're saying, the same thought crossed ma mind too; it's no ideal and no for you either. Let me think about it. Dinnae mention anything tae Michael or Clodagh and no tae the children either. I dinnae wish tae raise anyone's hopes, until I'm certain.

"Alright. But you're not saying no?" Ella checked with hope.

He nodded and kissed her forehead. "I'll give it much consideration, ye have ma word. Now can ye blow that candle out, I need tae sleep?"

She leaned over and blew it out, feeling pleased that he would at least consider the idea of staying in Ireland. It was comforting to know they had family nearby, if they did stay, and she could still visit Clodagh.

"Oh there you are, Ross called you again." Emily placed the receiver down and walked away from the telephone.

"What did he say?" Molly hung her coat up in the hallway and pulled off her muddy welly boots.

"He said he called to wish you a happy new year and he hopes that you have a good evening. Oh and that he's looking forward to you coming back in two days' time... not like he's counting or anything, is it?" Emily pulled a sorrowful face. "It's so sad. I've never even met the poor chap, but you can hear the desperation in his voice and I feel so sorry for him."

"Oh please don't make me feel worse than I already do... I need a cup of tea!"

Emily followed after her sister. "Only a cup of tea? You look like you need a stiff brandy."

"Believe me, I will tonight."

"Well I should hope so, seeing as it is New Year's Eve."

Molly placed the kettle under the tap, filled it up and then plonked it down on the stove, before lighting it and turning to face Emily again. "I've got to give him my answer tonight."

"Who, Adam or Ross?"

"Adam, of course."

"I take it by the look on your face, you haven't made up your mind then?"

Molly reached for two clean cups from the cupboard and put them on the table. "My head says stand by Adam, don't be a nincompoop and throw away what we once had, and my heart says I can't wait to be back with Ross." The look of torment was clear in her eyes.

"I'd be inclined to be a nincompoop and listen to your heart, it's where true feelings normally come from."

"Yes but the heart doesn't always lead one to making the right decision," Molly replied judiciously. "Adam has been through so much... he almost died." The story he told her about being found in a ditch by a farmer weighed heavily on her mind. If the farmer hadn't rescued him, even though it did seem a bizarre story, nevertheless, if he hadn't, Adam would not be alive and back home.

"You can't marry him because he almost died, Moll."

"I know that."

The kettle let off a piercing whistle and Molly quickly

took it off the stove.

"Let me do your hair for tonight." Emily smiled, in an attempt to cheer up her sister. "Soon you'll be back up in Scotland and it'll be ages before I see you again." There was sadness to her tone and Molly couldn't help but feel guilty for leaving again.

"A small smile appeared on Molly's lips. "Yes, you can do my hair. I've no idea what I'm going to wear though, I might have to raid your wardrobe."

"So what's new? You always do."

"I don't," she replied with a playful pout.

"Yes you do, Molly Moo!"

"Don't call me Molly Moo, you know I hate it!"

"What does she do?" Henry wandered into the kitchen, overhearing their conversation. "Oh good timing, I see you are making a brew especially for me."

"Steal my clothes," Emily replied. "And we weren't making a brew especially for you. Believe it or not, the world doesn't revolve around Henry Hazleton."

"Of course it does! Well she doesn't pinch my clothes, thankfully." Henry grinned and sat down at the table.

Molly placed another cup and the teapot on the table. "Of course I don't, your clothes wouldn't fit me, silly!" Molly said, trying to keep a straight face, looking at the pair of them. It was so good to be back home, she had missed their familiar banter and teasing, and she especially missed her girlie chats with Emily.

Molly frowned walking into the living room. Daphne was playing criss cross words with Charlie. "Are you not coming, Auntie?" Molly asked, noticing she wasn't dressed up.

"No. Who would babysit if I went?" Not that she wanted to go, she had made that clear to Ruth and George. She didn't feel comfortable around loud, drunk people making fools out of themselves just because one year was ending and another was beginning. Staying at home with Charlie, playing criss cross words in front of the fire, was far more appealing.

"I don't need babysitting," Charlie retorted, looking displeased.

"Of course you don't. What I meant to say was who would play criss cross words with Charlie if I went?" She winked at Molly and Molly smiled knowingly. "Well, I hope you both enjoy your evening." She bent over and kissed Daphne on the cheek and tried to do the same to Charlie but he ducked swiftly out of the way, not relishing the idea of a soppy kiss from his big sister.

"Oh Auntie, about what you said before, did you mean it... about Adam converting the outbuildings into stables?"

"Yes, if he's up to the job." She peered over the top of her spectacles at Molly. "Does this mean he's coming?"

"Molly! Come on!" George's booming voice echoed from outside. He was standing on the porch with Ruth and Emily, huddled together against the cold wanting to hurry up and walk to keep warm.

"I'll let you know in the morning. Best get going, father sounds impatient."

"Your father is always impatient," Daphne scoffed, pushing her glasses further up her nose and then looking back at the word board again. "Did you just cheat?"

"No!" Charlie giggled. For once he was actually enjoying being in his aunt's company, she seemed to be warming to him and wasn't as strict or as grumpy as she was last time she had come to stay, perhaps Molly had softened her.

The village hall was decked with bunting from one end to the other. In the corners were a multitude of colourful balloons and across the whole length of one wall, a banner read *Happy New Year, 1946!* Below it, a stage hosted a well-known local band playing a lively mix of jazz and swing. Everyone from the village and the surrounding hamlets were there. People danced and partied like never before, and for the first time in years they had something to really celebrate - the dawning of a new year, full of promise now that the war was finally over. The drinks flowed and the Hazletons mingled, danced and laughed. But by the time it got to 10.30pm, Molly cornered Emily with her concern about Adam's lack of appearance so far. "Do you think something bad has happened to Adam?"

"Like what, fallen down another ditch?" Emily swayed a little, steadying herself against the wall. The wine was going to her head. "Hey, perhaps he's waiting for a farmer to come and rescue him, or a farmer's daughter." She raised her brow and then giggled.

Molly shook her head. "Not funny!"

"Look on the bright side, at least you won't need to give him your answer, if he's not here to receive it." A tall fair haired lad, by the name of Harry who worked at the bakery, approached them nervously. Molly and Emily stared at him with curiosity, wondering which one of the sisters he was going to ask to dance. "Don't suppose you'd wanna dance?" His question was directed at Molly.

"Harry, is that really the way to ask a girl to dance?" Emily scoffed. Harry's face coloured.

"Sorry… I… I…" He became too flustered and so he turned to walk away. Molly, feeling sorry for him, grabbed his arm. "Harry, I'll dance with you."

His expression was one of astonishment. "Really? I mean great!" Without any further hesitation, he took Molly by the hand and led her to the dance floor, leaving

Emily giggling and swigging back the rest of her glass of wine, hoping someone would soon ask her to dance.

Molly only gave Harry the pleasure of one dance before making an excuse and disappearing out of sight. She glanced around the room. She could see her mum and dad chatting with friends, too busy to notice her. Henry looked sozzled, slouched on a chair in the corner of the room, chatting with some boy Molly didn't recognise, and Emily was now dancing with Jimmy Brown from the grocery store in the village. Grabbing her coat from the back of the chair where she had been sitting earlier, Molly walked outside.

The cold night air hit her at once and she found it quite exhilarating after the stifling heat from inside the hall. She checked her watch again - it was now just gone eleven o'clock. Why hadn't Adam turned up? It didn't make any sense. If he wanted to be together with her, as much as he said he did, surely he would be eager to hear her answer. She decided to make her way to his house. It was only a seven minute walk from the village hall and she wondered why she hadn't thought to go and call on him earlier, but then again, she didn't want to give the impression she was chasing him.

When she arrived, the house was in darkness. Adam's house was the end one in a row of six small cottages. Apart from one cottage in the middle, the rest were all in complete darkness, presumably because the inhabitants were all at the party. But of course, Adam's family wouldn't be at the party. She remembered him saying his parents and brother had gone away to visit a sick aunt in Cornwall. So if they had gone away without him and Adam wasn't at the party, where on earth was he? She knocked on the door anyway, on the off chance he might be there, perhaps he had fallen asleep. She banged her fist forcefully a few times on the wood, then stood back looking at the front door expectantly, waiting for it to suddenly open. It brought back memories being there again. She had not set foot in the Buxtons' home since before Adam had gone missing and she suddenly felt guilty for not making more of an effort to go and see Adam's family. What must have they thought of her not visiting them? Maybe if she had have gone to see them, it might have brought some kind of comfort to them all. But there was no point dwelling on the past; Adam was back now and they must be thrilled at him being home where he belonged. She wondered why they had not insisted he go with them to Cornwall after him being away for so long.

The door from the middle house with the only light burning flung open, interrupting her thoughts. An elderly woman in curlers and wearing a bright blue dressing gown and matching slippers, stood on the doorstep. "What are you doing banging on an empty house?" she called out. "No one's lived there in a long while."

Molly stared back at the woman feeling confused. "Are you saying the Buxtons have moved?"

"Yes, I am, love. Joy Buxton... she eh... well...she lost her marbles, bless her, after her son went missing and then the other one got killed - tragic affair it was, as with many families." Her voice trailed off momentarily in thought. "Anyway, she and her old man couldn't bear it no more, too many memories round here. They gave up the tenancy and moved out. Problem is it can't be rented out no more, got too much wrong with it you see, even those less fussy won't touch it, so it's been standing empty all this time."

"Sorry, did you say Graham Buxton, Adam's brother died?" Molly was trying desperately to catch up with the woman's rapid chatter.

"Yes, very sad it was. Anyway, haven't you got some

place to go with it being New Year? Young girl like you, I'd a thought you be at that party at the village hall."

"I was, but I was looking for Adam."

"Adam? Adam Buxton?" The woman now looked as baffled at Molly. "Did they find him then?"

"Yes," Molly nodded. "He's back home and he's safe and well."

"Oh thank goodness! It's so nice to hear a bit of good news and on New Year's Eve too. The Buxtons will be over the moon."

"Where have they moved to?" Molly asked, still puzzled.

"Somewhere near Pompey so I believe, they got family there you see."

"Portsmouth?" Molly said with surprise, "but that's miles away."

"I go to Pompey once a month to visit an old cousin of mine. It takes about forty five minutes on the bus if there's not much traffic." She shivered against the cold. "Look, I'd invite you in but it's getting late now and I'm not one for seeing the new year in, I'd sooner be tucked up in bed, me arthritis is playing up." She squeezed her left knee and grimaced as if proving a point.

"No it's fine. Don't worry, I have to go back to the party, but thank you for telling me all this, it's very helpful."

The woman nodded and went back indoors, relieved to be getting out of the cold. Molly, mulling over her conversation with the old woman, walked back down the street in the direction of the village hall. None of it made any sense. Adam had said his brother had lost an arm not that he had died, and why didn't he say he was now living in Portsmouth? Then it dawned on her about the buses. Perhaps that's why he couldn't come to the party, the buses were probably not running on New Year's Eve and if they were, they certainly wouldn't be running late enough for him to get home. But that still didn't account for why he had agreed to come to the party in the first place if he didn't have transport.

She could see the inviting lights of the hall and could hear the music and laughter that echoed around the village. She glanced at her watch; it was almost midnight. No point waiting any longer for Adam, he was obviously not coming. She pushed open the door and went back inside.

From the field opposite, Adam watched Molly go back to the party. Dressed in black, he sat down on the wall opposite and listened to the noise of people making merriment, wiping away his tears with gloved hands, and wishing more than anything he could be there with Molly enjoying himself like everyone else was. And as he sat contemplating what kind of future lay ahead for him, the church bell in the village chimed twelve times, followed by an outcry of Happy New Year from within the village hall, and the band played Auld Lang Syne. From where he was sitting, through the window he could see everyone linking arms, dancing and singing. He shivered against the cold, stood up and with his head hung low, he walked away into the darkness.

Chapter Three

Henry put the suitcases in the boot of the car. Molly came out with a large bag and handed it to him. "Mother seems to think there are no shops in Scotland!"

"Of course there are, but full of whisky and tartan scarves!" He turned to face her with a grin. "Well Sis, try not to get into any more trouble up there. No visiting the Ghost Tree, not without me anyway."

"I told you - I'm not doing that anymore, it messes with my head and God knows I've had enough of that recently."

"Yes, you have. I'm sorry about Adam," Henry said, sounding genuinely sincere for once.

"Yes well…" She shuffled awkwardly on the spot.

"He'll be sorry whenever I see him again," George said, walking towards the car. "Messing my daughter around like that, turning up out of the blue then standing her up on New Year's Eve."

"Dad, I'm fine, honestly."

"You would say that. You're good at putting on a brave face - you're a Hazleton. We all know how to bury our feelings very well." He closed the boot and got into the car ready to drive them to the train station.

The rest of the family piled out of the farmhouse wanting to wave them off. Daphne said a brief farewell, since she wasn't one for goodbyes or anything that would trigger any kind of real emotion and show a side to her that no one was accustomed to. She got into the back of the car. She felt safer in the back rather than riding in the front, and preferred not to sit too close to George; she'd heard more than enough of his opinionated views on anything and everything, all over the Christmas holiday.

"I suppose I'm back to milking the goats then!" Charlie huffed.

"I'm afraid so, little brother." Molly leaned forward to kiss him and he ducked, so she grabbed hold of him tightly and kissed his cheek while he squealed like a piglet, and the others laughed.

Emily hugged her sister. "For the record," she said, whispering in Molly's ear. "I think Ross is the one. I never liked Adam much anyway."

"You changed your tune. You were the one telling me to give him a chance at Christmas."

"Yeah well he blew that chance."

Ruth held out her arms, welling up again for the third time that morning. She hated saying goodbye, she missed Molly dreadfully and wished they'd had more time to chat alone. "Don't rush into anything with the gardener." She still had her doubts about Ross after what Daphne had told her, filling Molly's head about some magic tree that can make people see their past lives. The boy was obviously a bit of a dreamer.

"He has a name, Mum. You don't need to refer to him as *the gardener*."

"Right, sorry, Ross the gardener then," she smiled wryly. "Shall we just send Adam packing if he turns up? I mean he could have been taken ill, I suppose, and that's why he hasn't been back?" She felt she should give him the benefit of the doubt, given he was engaged to Molly and he had been through an awful lot.

"Give him the telephone number at Aberdoch Manor, if he does show his face. I'll speak to him on the phone, at least he can give me the explanation I'm owed."

"Molly, you never did tell us what your answer would

have been on New Year's Eve, had he turned up," Ruth said thoughtfully.

Emily listened with interest, wanting to know too. Charlie had gone to the car to see the others, bored with the conversation.

Molly sighed. "I was going to say yes, for him to come to Scotland and for us to make a go of it."

"Oh darling, I'm so sorry," Ruth hugged her again.

"Molly, get a shift on or you'll miss the train!" George shouted out of the car window.

"It's alright, Mum, I think he did me a favour. I think it's for the best. I felt duty bound agreeing to him coming to Scotland, but I'm not sure my heart was really in it, in fact, I know it wasn't."

"You dodged a bullet!" Emily planted another kiss on her sister's cheek.

Benji gave a short bark and Molly knelt down and made a quick fuss of him before dashing off towards the car.

A forceful wind was blowing up dust from the pavement. Ella held on tightly to her bonnet with one hand and with the other she brought her cape closer around her neck. Hooves echoed back and forth and the wheels of carriages rattled along the cobbles, as people went about their business in all directions. It was exhilarating being in the hustle and bustle of Dublin after the quietness of Oaklands in Tallaght, tucked away on the outskirts. She stopped in her tracks and her eyes strayed to an imposing grey stone building on the other side of the road. It was a modern build, around ten or eleven years old, with many large windows, and steps leading up to a big black door. Out of curiosity, Ella crossed the road, dodging the many carriages. She stood at the foot of the steps and looked up. Not being able to resist finding out what the building was used for, she walked up the steps and went inside. Wandering through a spacious foyer, to the left, she noticed a door slightly ajar and so she pushed it open and entered a long, narrow room with rows of beds of sick people lined up on either side of the walls. At the far end, a fire was lit, although not beneficial to those closest to the door.

A middle-aged plump and rosy-cheeked woman, wearing a dark coloured gown and a white apron to match her head dress covering her peppery coloured hair, approached Ella. "Are you here to see someone?"

"No, sorry, I was just curious. I didn't realise it was a…" Her gaze drifted to a young woman in the corner who seemed to be distressed by her swollen throat. She opened her mouth in attempt to gain more air and held out her bright red tongue.

"Hospital," the nurse replied, finishing off Ella's sentence for her. "This is Mercer's Hospital. The sign outside blew down in a recent storm and it's still not been replaced."

"That lady, does she have scarlet fever?" Ella asked, dragging her attention back to the conversation.

"Yes, she does. Do you have knowledge of this illness?" The nurse held Ella's gaze, curious about this English woman taking such an interest.

"Yes, I have. I have experience with healing people," Ella confirmed.

"What type of experience?" The nurse narrowed her eyes, scrutinising Ella closely.

"I ran a small apothecary in my village in England. I provided healing for many of the locals and I also travelled with the Jacobite, healing the injured. My husband is a Jacobite supporter, you see."

"The Jacobite?" The nurse raised an eyebrow with surprise. "Most people certainly support the cause around these parts." Her face softened with a small smile. She liked the girl, she seemed sincere and to detect scarlet fever at a distance, she must be very knowledgeable. "Are you looking for work?" she asked with hope.

Ella's face lit up. "Yes, yes I am." The words had left her mouth before she could even think, but what was there to think about? She missed healing the sick and now she had just been given the opportunity, handed to her quite by accident but she took it as a sign that it was meant to be.

"The pay is pittance, I warn you."

"I don't mind that. I'd be happy to help in any way I can."

"What's your name?"

"Jane Fergus," she lied. It was better to be safe than sorry.

"Amelia Murphy." She held out her hand and Ella accepted the gesture.

"Well, Jane Fergus, let me show you around.

"Wonderful!" Ella beamed excitedly.

Joan unlocked the front door of the vicarage while Norman collected the shopping bags from the car. No sooner had the front door opened, Carrot, their old, ginger and white cat, having waited patiently to get inside for over an hour while Joan and Norman had been shopping, dashed inside, nearly knocking Joan off her feet. "Carrot, one of these days I'll break my neck over you!"

"Vicar!" Norman turned around to see Ross running towards him.

"Ross," Norman greeted him with a wave, watching him as he came closer, trying to catch his breath. "Something wrong, Ross?"

"Aye, there is." He pushed his fingers anxiously through a mop of auburn curls. "Aberdoch Manor is flooded. I noticed water pouring out from under the front door. I managed tae find the water mains which, luckily, were outside and I turned them off, but I've no idea of the state inside."

"Oh dear that doesn't sound good. Don't you have a key for the house?" Norman asked, while placing the shopping bags just inside the front door. He turned towards Ross again, presuming that he hadn't or he would have used it.

"No I don't, I was hoping you had one?"

Norman shook his head. "Mrs Winters wouldn't leave a key with me."

Ross frowned. "Whyever not? You're trustworthy - you're a vicar!"

"Which means absolutely nothing to Daphne Winters, I can assure you." He blinked several times and pushed his glasses back up his nose. Just saying Daphne's name out loud made him twitch.

"Perhaps she has a spare key hidden at the back of the house," Ross said, pensively, wondering why he had not thought of that in the first place. He had checked under the plant pots in the porch, and had left no stone unturned. "I have the telephone number of where they are in Hampshire, Molly gave it to me," he continued. "I think they should know what's happening, although," he checked his watch, "they are due back today, so they could have left already."

Norman looked at his watch too. "Oh yes, if they're back later today they probably are on their way, but no harm in trying. Come inside."

"What's up?" Joan asked, picking up the last of the shopping bags from the hallway to take into the kitchen. "Hello Ross," she greeted him with a friendly smile.

"Aberdoch Manor has been flooded and Ross is going to call Mrs Winters in Hampshire," Norman informed her.

"Goodness. Well let me put this away and then I think we should go and take a look." She dashed off in the direction of the kitchen, not waiting for their reply.

A 16th century tower house with arched windows stood central to the sprawling grey stone buildings either side of it - they had been added over the years around a sizeable courtyard. The property was surrounded by extensive gardens that Ross had been busy working on for almost four months, and despite the harsh winter they had experienced so far, it was starting to take shape.

Water could be seen trickling from underneath the large wooden front door, out onto the porch and down the steps. Norman's old Austin pulled up in front of the steps and the three of them bundled out of the vehicle.

"So, you didn't manage to get hold of Mrs Winters on the phone when you called her?" Joan asked, looking over at the water that had made it as far down as the path next to the car.

"No. Molly's mum answered and said they were on their way. The train gets into Eyemouth at five o'clock," Ross replied, feeling excited at the prospect of seeing Molly again, although concerned that she may have been avoiding his calls, either that or she was just extremely busy. But he had hoped she had missed him and as much as he had missed her, at least enough to speak to him on the phone.

"Well it's good that you've managed to turn the water off from the mains," Norman said, avoiding a puddle next to his feet. "Check the porch again for a key and I'll go around the back and look through the window." He left Joan and Ross to search and rushed off down the side of the house. Arriving outside of the kitchen window, he peered in and could see a river of brown, mucky water all over the kitchen floor, flowing out of the room and into the hallway. He checked all around, under plant pots, stones and rocks but there was no key. Joan and Ross appeared at his side. "Doesn't seem to be a key anywhere," Joan said with a small groan of frustration.

Norman took a large stone from the garden and then went back and smashed the glass in the back door. He had a sense of déjà vu wash over him. He had done the exact same thing in December when there had been a snowstorm and he had rescued Henry from the lane, sitting in the snow and drinking whisky after hurting his ankle trying to make his way to Aberdoch Manor. Norman had helped him through the storm, but when they arrived at Aberdoch Manor, the house was in darkness. He saw a man through the study window, dressed in a kilt and holding a sword. Norman, in his panic to save Daphne and Molly, had broken the back door and let himself in, only to find that Daphne and Molly were well and playing cards. When he questioned them about the intruder in the study, they had told him he had seen the spirit of Fergus McDaniel, a warrior from two hundred years ago. What nonsense. Norman shook his head at the silly explanation they had given him. He never did find out who the intruder was.

Thankful that he had welly boots on, he stepped into the kitchen, followed by Joan and Ross right behind him.

"Gracious!" Joan grimaced. "We are going to have to try and get this water outside.

"I'll get some buckets, brooms and anything else that might be of use from the shed," Ross said.

Chapter Four

The train chugged into Eyemouth station, letting off a deafening whistle. It came to a grinding halt and the platform became lost in several puffs of smoke. The carriage doors opened and passengers disembarked. Molly placed their luggage down then offered Daphne a hand, helping her off the train. They made their way through the crowds.

Norman, being extremely tall, spotted them in the distance. He made his way towards them, in his normal ungainly manner, jostling from side to side as he pushed through, apologising profusely. At last he reached them. "Mrs Winters." He pasted on a courteous smile, doing his best to compose himself.

"What are *you* doing here?" Daphne pursed her lips, eyeing him up and down disdainfully.

"Vicar Norman, how nice of you to meet us. How did you know which train we were on?" Molly asked, baffled to see him, unlike Daphne, who found his presence as always, irksome.

"I'm afraid I have some bad news," he said, looking at them both through his thick, black-rimmed glasses. "It seems there's been a flood at Aberdoch Manor... a burst pipe by the looks of it."

"What?" Daphne's brow creased.

"How bad is it?" Molly asked, placing the heavy suitcases down on the platform.

"Quite bad," he grimaced. "But only downstairs, upstairs is fine," he added quickly, in an attempt to reassure them.

"How do you know all this?" Daphne narrowed her eyes at him. "Don't tell me you broke in again."

"Auntie, you make Vicar Norman sound like a common burglar."

Daphne harrumphed. "Well, if the cap fits."

"Unfortunately, as neither myself nor Ross had a key..."

"Well of course not," Daphne cut in scornfully.

"Ross? Was Ross with you?" Saying his name gave Molly flutters of excitement in her belly, despite the unfortunate situation of the flood.

"Yes. Ross noticed the water flooding out from under the front door. He managed to find the mains, which were outside, and switched them off. But we needed to get inside to assess how bad it was and try and clean it up as much as possible for your return."

"How sweet of you," said Molly.

"So, how did you get in?" Daphne folded her arms defiantly. "Don't tell me, you broke the blessed kitchen door again. You have, haven't you?"

"I'm afraid so," Norman blinked hard. "But I'll pay to get it repaired, like I did before."

"It's not your fault, you were only trying to help, just like it wasn't your fault before." Molly gave a sideways look of distaste at Daphne.

"Well, anyway... um... myself, Joan and Ross worked as hard as we could to shovel the water out but I'm afraid we couldn't manage to get it all out in time for your arrival. Ross called your home in Hampshire and your mum," he said, looking at Molly, trying to keep his attention off Daphne, due to her making him feel so very uncomfortable, "your mum said you had already left."

"Well, thank you for trying to clean it up," Molly said. "I suppose we should find a hotel in Eyemouth, don't you think Auntie, and then see the damage in the morning?"

"Oh no, it's fine," Norman interrupted. "Joan insists that you come and stay with us for the night."

"Oh does she now?" Daphne shook her head. "And let me guess, she's making one of her casseroles?"

"Auntie, please." Molly threw her a daggered look.

"That's really kind of you both and we…"

"We'd rather stay in a hotel," Daphne continued.

Molly's face flushed at Daphne's rudeness. "It's probably for the best." She couldn't bear putting poor Norman and Joan through another evening with Daphne, not after last time. She had no idea why Daphne had such a dislike to them both. They were decent, nice enough people, a little judgemental at times but they meant well and were extremely kind.

"Very well." Norman tried his best to conceal his relief. "At least let me drive you into Eyemouth and help you find a suitable hotel. I can pick you up in the morning and you can see the damage in daylight."

"Thank you Vicar Norman," Molly smiled, appreciating his help, even if Daphne didn't.

Daphne reluctantly nodded her head in agreement. At least it would save her in taxi fares. She didn't want Norman to have any part of helping them out. The man was infuriating, but what was more infuriating right now was the flood and she wondered about the cost involved, and the amount of work it would take to get the house repaired, ready for the opening of the hotel.

Norman reached down and picked up the suitcases. "Ross said to say hello." Norman glanced back over his shoulder at Molly. "He would have come with me but I was unsure about how much luggage you would have, so he said he will see you tomorrow."

Molly beamed. She couldn't wait to see him, although she was still contemplating if she should tell him about

Adam's return. It seemed the right thing to do. She wanted to be honest with Ross. And as Adam seemed to have decided not to want to be with her after all, she supposed their engagement was now off, for which she couldn't help but feel relieved. It was most bizarre, a year ago, even six months ago, she would have been thrilled at Adam's return but since meeting Ross, her feelings for Adam had changed, even more so now he had made no effort to see her since Boxing Day and had stood her up on New Year's Eve. Perhaps he didn't feel the same way either anymore. They had been apart for a very long time and so much had happened, it was always going to be hard to pick up where they left off.

Joan opened the front door as Norman parked in the driveway. "Were they not on the train? You've been ages." She stood in the doorway with her hands on her hips.

"They were on the train, alright," he said, heading towards her. "They, well Daphne Winters, didn't want to stay with us." He gave her a peck on the cheek and she moved out of the way so that he could go indoors.

"Why? I've made a casserole, especially." Joan followed him into the living room looking as perplexed as she sounded.

"You know what that woman is like. Anyway, I'm relieved, to be honest." He sat down in his favourite armchair and closed his eyes, happy to be home at last. It had been a long day, what with an early morning meeting at the church about fundraising for the repair of the roof, shopping with Joan, shovelling water out of Aberdoch Manor, then picking Daphne and Molly up from the train station and hunting for hotels around Eyemouth. After visiting four different hotels, Daphne decided she preferred the first one they looked at after all as it had better views over the harbour.

"Where are they staying? They've not gone back to Aberdoch Manor, surely?"

"No. They're at a hotel in Eyemouth. I wished the hotel manager the best of luck as I left them in the foyer, goodness knows he'll need it!"

"Norman!" Joan stifled a giggle, sitting down on the sofa opposite. "I've made plenty of food. I suppose they can always have it when they return."

"As long as I don't have to deliver it," Norman moaned. Carrot made a beeline for his lap, taking him by surprise as the cat's paws landed on Norman's bony thighs. "Ouch!" Carrot, ignoring his objection, purred loudly, circling for a moment before positioning himself comfortably, ready for a long snooze.

"Looks like you won't be going anywhere for a while," Joan smiled, pointing at Carrot. "I'll make you a cup of tea and we'll have dinner a bit later if you want, give you time to relax a bit."

"Um, thank you," Norman mumbled and then yawned. No sooner had Joan left the room, he fell asleep.

It was eight o'clock when they sat down for dinner, the same as every evening, allowing time for Michael and Fergus to return from the mill. The candlelight shone a glow over the silverware and crystal glasses. They dug into a hearty meal of pheasant and a variation of roasted vegetables, cooked to perfection as always by Mrs O'Connor, the cook.

"I have some news," Ella announced.

Clodagh smiled knowingly. Ella had not been able to contain her excitement when she had returned home earlier that day, and now she was bursting with enthusiasm.

"Oh, and what might that be?" Fergus' eyes gleamed with amusement. Perhaps she had managed to persuade Mrs O'Connor to let her bake a cake after all. But her news wasn't as trivial as he had expected.

"I visited a hospital today, Mercer's Hospital in Dublin and, well, they would like me to help them," she smiled broadly, feeling proud.

There was a stunned silence as both Fergus and Michael realised the potential consequences of her working in a busy hospital in the centre of Dublin. Fergus stared back at Ella in disbelief, but it was Michael who spoke first. "Mercer's Hospital started life as a shelter for poor girls back in 1724. About twelve years ago some well-known surgeons took it over, making it into a hospital. I ken one of the board of governors, Jonathan Swift. It's a good and decent organisation but Ella, do ye think it wise you being there, given the circumstances?"

"Why would it not be wise? And what circumstances?" Clodagh sat forward, looking directly at her husband, bemused.

"Of course it is no wise, it's far from wise," Fergus replied, meeting Ella's eyes challengingly.

"Whyever not?" Clodagh pressed, unable to comprehend his seemingly unjust reaction.

"Because she is with child," Fergus replied coolly, before Michael could reply. This was only part of the reason of course. The fact that she was exposing herself to the danger of being recognised was another, but not one he could share with Clodagh. It seemed that Michael had kept his word and not told Clodagh, which was why she failed to understand the implications of Ella working at Mercer's hospital. He was thankful to his cousin. The less people that knew, the better.

"I said I would only help two or three days a week. They are fully aware of my condition," Ella replied in her defence. "If I feel tired, I will leave."

Fergus glared at her from across the table, livid that she should put herself and the family in jeopardy, and furthermore, not even realise she was doing so. "You'll no be working there, and I will not hear another word on the matter." His voice was low and precise and his eyes showed he meant business. She bowed her head, trying to contain her tears as she continued to eat. Had they been alone, she would have protested profusely, but it was not respectful to make a scene in front of Michael and Clodagh. She would need to wait until later to make her feelings clear, and she was determined to have her say.

An awkward silence descended on the table, other than the clinking of cutlery as they ate and the ticking of the clock on the far side of the room. At last, Michael resumed conversation once more about the mill, gaining Fergus' attention regarding the practicalities of a meeting they were to attend tomorrow with a potential client. Clodagh patted Ella's hand with affection, and Ella forced a small smile of gratitude. At least Clodagh understood how much she missed her work and her need to feel useful again. Being a healer was a vocation and she couldn't contemplate a life without helping others.

Fergus and Ella retired to their bedroom early. It was clear they wanted to be alone and to resolve their differences. Michael and Clodagh remained in the drawing-room while they finished their drink before bed.

"I do feel sorry for Ella," Clodagh said, wriggling against the cushion behind her back, trying to find some comfort against her backache. "It's a grand opportunity for her to work at the hospital, putting her skills to good use."

"I daresay it is, but Fergus has a point. I'd be worried if it were you, working while carrying my child." He took a swig of whisky and stretched out his long legs, understanding the need not to tell her the full story. It wasn't that he didn't trust her, but he didn't wish to burden her with problems that weren't hers to be burdened with.

"Michael, how do you think the working class cope? The women work until they drop and the next day, they are back again continuing their duties."

"Ella is no longer working class, she's married to Fergus now, she has status… she's a McDaniel. I thought you of all people should understand that."

"Meaning what precisely, me of all people?" She looked annoyed at him.

"That it's not proper for a lady to work, everyone kens that. Anyway, I'm tired, I'm going tae turn in." He stood up and walked over to her, placing a dutiful kiss on her cheek. She grabbed his hand and held it tightly. "Let's not quarrel, this is not about us."

He sighed heavily. "Of course. I love you, ye ken that." This time he kissed her tenderly on the lips.

"Of course I wouldn't put us in danger," Ella retorted, sitting on the edge of the bed. "I haven't even told them my real name. I said it was Jane Fergus. They know nothing about me and I won't tell them either."

Fergus picked up an iron prong and poked the fire, he placed it back down by the side of the fireplace and turned to face her again. "And what happens when someone recognises you from a wanted poster?"

"There are no wanted posters for me here in Dublin."

"Yet!" he replied sharply, knowing he was clutching

at straws and probably being overprotective but it was his duty to make sure no harm came to her.

"Fergus, I feel lost here, like a fish out of water." She wiped away a stray tear that trickled down her left cheek. Lilly is happy playing with Mary every day, she'll be fine here with Clodagh. Ian is with you at the mill all day. I need to fill my time being useful as I have always done. When the baby comes, I know I won't be able to work as a healer, I'll be too busy. Please don't take away this opportunity from me." She watched him with pleading eyes.

He came towards her and sat down next to her on the bed. "Ye ken I dinnae want tae take this opportunity away from you." He took her hand into his own and looked her in the eyes. "I cannae bear it if they took you and the bairn away from me." He glided a gentle hand over her tummy.

"And they won't. They are not even looking for me here. The moment I suspect anything suspicious, or you see one poster for me, I'll leave the hospital immediately."

He sighed heavily. It was hopeless and he hated arguing with her. "I'll agree tae two days a week and only for six weeks. I dinnae want you putting yer health and the baby's at risk."

A broad smile broke upon Ella's lips. "Agreed!" She stroked the side of his face with affection. "And I promise I will be very careful."

"You'd better be or I'll have tae put you over ma knee, Ella McDaniel," he said with a grin. He couldn't be angry with her for long, and he knew just how much she wanted this opportunity. After everything she had gone through, how could he deprive her of a little happiness? Try as he might to not feel guilty, he still did and probably would for the rest of his life. He had led Ella back to Aberdoch

Manor without checking the facts that she was properly pardoned for the crimes she was accused of. They had been safe staying with Aunt Ava on the Isle of Arran, and he had been too quick to leave. He had not been on his guard enough to recognise the signs that the McKenzies were planning their attack, nor did he suspect Andrew McCabe's disloyalty. He could have stopped all of this, Shona's death, all the heartache he had put the children through and Ella too, had he been cautious and not acted on impulse. It was a hard lesson to learn but now he was determined not to make the same mistake again. He would protect his family no matter what.

"Ross left your wellies out for you," Norman said as they walked up muddy steps covered in leaves to the front door of Aberdoch Manor.

"He's so thoughtful." Molly smiled, gazing over at the garden, but Ross hadn't arrived for work yet.

Daphne retrieved the key from her handbag and opened the door. She had been uncharacteristically quiet in the car, contemplating the work and expense, should the insurance not cover it all and wondering just how much damage had been done.

The damp and the smell of mildew hit her nostrils the moment the door opened. She looked down at the mud-stained carpets with a large sigh. Puddles of water could be seen in various areas where the carpet had not completely absorbed it. Norman poked his head inside, keeping his feet dry on the front porch.

"I've a good plumber who helped with some problems

at the vicarage. This is his telephone number." Norman handed the piece of paper to Daphne.

"Right," she sniffed, still busy looking at the state of the new carpet that had been fitted only a month ago.

"I've had the kitchen door repaired. A chap came first thing this morning and sorted it."

She glanced up at him and nodded.

He didn't expect a thank you from Daphne, but at least she accepted the telephone number of the plumber and acknowledged the repaired kitchen door without any insolent remarks.

"I have forewarned the plumber that you may be contacting him today and he would need to attend to the job urgently," Norman concluded.

The telephone rang, startling them both, forcing an end to Norman's nervous chatter.

"At least the telephone is working," Molly said, in an attempt to sound positive for Daphne's sake if not her own. She stood next to Norman on the porch peering inside.

Daphne squelched across to answer the persistent ringing telephone, pulling a face with each footstep as the water seeped into her shoes.

"Auntie, you should have let me answer, I'm wearing boots." Molly pointed down at the wellies she had just slipped her feet into, having left her shoes on the steps.

"If you want to go back to the hotel, I'll gladly pick you both up later today and drive you," Norman offered, pushing his glasses back up his nose.

"Thank you, but we have the truck and I can drive us back to Eyemouth if need be. I suppose it just depends on how much we can get done today and if its habitable enough for us to stay here tonight." Molly glanced to her right in the direction of the living room, the murky trickles of water could be seen entering the room. She wondered what state it was in, and if the sofas and chairs would be damaged.

"Yes Ruth, I know that and the insurance..." Daphne continued her chatter in the background.

"Molly!" Ross called out, dashing across the courtyard and up the steps, sweeping her off her feet the moment he reached her. She shrieked with excitement. Anyone would think they hadn't seen each other for months, yet she had only been gone just over a week.

"I'll be off then," Norman said, making a swift exit. It was clear he wasn't needed anymore by either Daphne or Molly. Molly didn't notice him walk away, get in his car or drive off, she was far too busy hugging and kissing.

"I'm so sorry ye had tae come back tae all this," Ross said at last, pointing towards the open front door. Daphne stood with her back to the door, still busy talking.

"Thank goodness you managed to stop the water and get most of it out, we're really grateful."

His eyes were fixed on hers. "I've missed you so much. You must have been very busy. I only spoke tae ye once the whole time ye were in Hampshire, it almost killed me."

"I know and I'm really sorry." She suddenly felt consumed with guilt. How could she had even contemplated bringing Adam back with her, it would have broken Ross' heart."

He noticed her forlorn expression. "Hey, it's alright. I understand you were busy with your family."

"I have so much to tell you but it will have to wait until later, I'm afraid." She needed to tell him about Adam, that he had come back, but now was not the right time. Furthermore, she wanted to think about just how much she was willing to tell him and would she be able to find the courage to say she was going to bring him to Aberdoch Manor had he had turned up on New Year's

Eve? Then again, did he really need to know all the details, especially now she was back in Scotland miles away from Adam and Hampshire?

"Of course, there's no rush. Let me help. The garden can wait, I can work on the house with you today, help clean it up."

"Well you can start by putting the kettle on then," Daphne instructed, placing the receiver back down. "Your mother can talk the hind legs off a donkey." She wiggled a finger in her right ear and then walked away from the telephone table with exaggerated steps, looking like she had messed herself. Molly and Ross did their best to contain their amusement, holding hands and happy to be reunited again.

Chapter Five

At sunrise, Charlie entered the goat pen to milk the goats before he headed off to school. Unaware that he was being watched from the mezzanine above lined with bales of straw, he grabbed a tin bucket and pulled up a small stool, sitting down next to the first goat, which was one of six that needed milking. He rubbed his hands together, the black and white goat let out a string of bleats in protest as Charlie wrapped his small hand around one of the udders and squeezed. His palms weren't quite warm enough it seemed. It was when he was milking the third goat that he heard a scraping noise above his head and then saw a pair of tanned, scuffed ankle boots appear on the ladder. He jumped up from fright and then gazed upwards to see Adam heading down the ladder towards him. "What are you doing here? Have you got some kind of death wish? If my Dad sees you, he'll kill you."

"Well, he's not here, is he?" Adam's eyes darted around the pen, as if checking George wasn't suddenly going to appear from behind the goats. "I need to ask you a favour," he said, looking back at Charlie, while brushing straw from his jacket. He looked dishevelled, having not shaved for a few days.

"Have you been sleeping up there?" Charlie screwed up his eyes suspiciously at Adam.

"Only last night. I'm having some trouble at home," he admitted.

"What kind of trouble?"

"Never you mind," he replied sharply, not wishing to

divulge any more information.

"Is that why you didn't come to see our Molly?" Charlie continued. "She was dead upset, you know."

"I know and I'm really sorry about that. I want to make it up to her but she's gone, so I need to know where this mansion is that she's staying at in Scotland, the one your aunt is turning into a hotel," he added unnecessarily.

"And why should I tell you? Everyone hates your guts for hurting her, and they'll hate mine 'n' all if I tell you where she is." He gave Adam the once over from head to toe. "Anyway, by the state of you, looks like you couldn't afford the train fare, even if I did tell you."

"I've got money," Adam replied, sounding insulted. "Enough to get me to Scotland. And your aunt has offered me a job, apparently, so it'll be no problem once I'm up there."

"That was before you stood our Molly up on New Year's Eve. She won't want to give you a job now."

Adam pulled out a shiny, hexagonal, brass coin, ignoring Charlie's last comment. "I got this in France," he said, holding his palm out for Charlie to see.

Charlie's eyes immediately lit up. He had a collection of old coins his grandfather had left him, some of them dating back to the early 1800s.

"It's two French Francs. This coin only came out three years ago."

"Wow!" You know, I have a Reichsmark that Henry gave me. He found it on a dead Jerry and brought it back with him." His eyes gleamed fervently.

"Great! Well now you can have this coin too, if you tell me where your sister is staying?" Adam pasted on his best beguiling smile.

Charlie sighed. The temptation was great, he had to admit. "If I tell you, do you promise not to say it was me what told you?"

Adam placed his right palm on his chest. "Hand on heart, you have my word, I promise."

"Well, give me the coin and I'll tell you," Charlie held out his hand.

"Not so fast!" He put it on the stool next to where he stood. "There, once you tell me you can grab it."

"Alright. It's called Aberdoch Manor, it's in a place called Aberdoch but I couldn't tell you where that is. Henry said it was in the middle of nowhere. And he also said it was as cold as the North Pole and everyone speaks funny up there, you can't understand a word they say.

Adam grinned. "I'm sure I'll cope. There, get your coin and you better get back to them goats."

Charlie nodded, grabbing it from the stool. He took a moment to inspect it with awe and then stuffed it inside his pocket, realising he was going to be late for school if he didn't hurry up with the milking.

The machines worked relentlessly, clattering and banging, driven by men and boys, turning raw material into paper. At one end of the mill, the deliveries arrived, consisting of rags, grass and wood pulp. And from the other end, paper of all sizes and qualities were loaded up to be taken away and sold. Over a hundred men and boys worked long hours but the working conditions were not bad. Michael McDaniel paid a fair wage, although it was far from a fortune, and he allowed them one day off a week. It was run systematically; everyone knew what was expected of them and they carried out their duties accordingly. They seemed to get on with work and appeared not to mind it, which was more than could be said for other workplaces in Dublin, where hard labour was nothing more than slavery.

Ian was working his way through a stack of old garments considered to be rags by their owners. He delved his hands inside the pockets of various clothing such as jackets and trousers. They were normally empty but sometimes he'd find a coin or something of even more value. Last week he had found an expensive looking watch and only yesterday a gold chain. Michael had strict rules when it came to personal belongings being found. They were to be handed in and kept safe in his office in case the owner realised they were missing and came looking for them. He prided himself on running an honest, decent business. And if after six months, no one had claimed the valuables, they could be pawned and the money used to treat the staff at Christmas.

Despite the noise coming from behind him, Ian heard banging on the side door close to where he was standing. He pushed the heavy, steel door open to find a pretty girl, no more than a year or two older than himself, standing with a sack of clothes in her hands.

"Mam said I was to drop these off to you." Her pale blue eyes clouded with tears as she looked up and handed him the sack. "They were me dah's clothes, he passed a month ago."

"Sorry tae hear that." Ian swallowed hard, feeling sympathetic towards the girl. "I ken what it feels like tae lose a loved one only too well."

She watched him, surprised by his Scottish accent and also that he too was no stranger to death. "Has your dah died too?" She searched his face, waiting for his reply.

"Aye and ma mam." A contagious sadness swept over him.

"You're an orphan, so you are then." She frowned. "Why aren't you at the workhouse?"

"My aunt and uncle are looking after me and ma sister, and ma cousin is the owner of this mill.

Ian hadn't noticed Fergus approaching.

"Mr McDaniel is your cousin?" Her eyes grew wide with astonishment. "So do you live in that big fancy house... Oaklands?"

"Aye, I do," Ian smiled, feeling grateful for his good fortune. "For now, anyhow."

"Ian!" Fergus rushed towards him, ending their conversation abruptly.

"Thank you, miss. You can be on yer way now." The girl nodded, realising she had outstayed her welcome - after all, a paper mill was no place for a girl and she shouldn't have been talking to the boy in the first place, even if he was Scottish, handsome and related to Mr McDaniel. Her mother would have scolded her if she knew.

"Sorry Uncle, I didnae..."

"You didnae think, no." Fergus chided. "Ye ken ye're no supposed tae tell folk too much about us. Where you live and who ye live with is none of her concern."

"Aye, Uncle, I understand." Ian hung his head, ashamed that he had broken Fergus' number one rule, not to speak to strangers about his private life.

"It's alright, lad, I suppose ye meant well." He ruffled his nephew's hair affectionately and walked off, feeling a tad guilty for being hard on him, but it was for his own good and for the good of all of them. It was important they kept a low profile as much as possible. Michael had not introduced Fergus or Ian to the workforce formally. As far as everyone was concerned, Fergus and Ian were probably father and son and had been seeking employment, and what with Michael being Scottish himself, he had felt sorry for them and given them both a job. With so much noise from all the machinery, idle chit chat could only be done after work and both Fergus and Ian always left the premises as quickly as possible at the end of the working day, giving no time to make friends with their colleagues. Most thought their aloofness was due to their being Scottish and living in a foreign land, needing time to adapt to their surroundings, while others didn't really care what their reason was for taking distance.

The fire crackled gently, giving a warm glow as Clodagh sat reading in her favourite armchair. Ella startled her with her sudden entrance.

"Sorry, I didn't mean to give you a fright." Ella flashed an apologetic smile, taking off her cape as the warmth of the room hit her skin.

"Oh, don't worry, I'm away with the fairies when I read, it's like the world doesn't exist," she grinned.

"What are you reading?"

"The Letters of Sarah Scott, a rather witty Anglican philanthropist."

"Oh, sounds intriguing," Ella said, having never heard of the author.

"How was your day? I'm dying to hear all about it." She placed a worn leather bookmark on the page she was reading and closed the book tightly.

"It was both interesting and impressive," Ella beamed, sitting down opposite on the sofa. "There were cupboards full of gleaming, glass bottles of all sizes containing all types of potions, plus stacks of clean bandages and compresses. The apothecary's cabinet is extremely organised with such a wide variety of herbs to choose from." She held out her palms in front of the fire to warm them. "There were dried leaves, roots and fungi, all neatly packed into gauze bags ready for immediate use. As I opened the cabinet, the spicy odour hit me." She inhaled, closing her eyes, remembering the scent very clearly, it reminded her of home when she had first started learning about herbs and remedies. "And the whole place is extremely clean, wherever you look."

"Well, that certainly does sound impressive, as one should expect from a hospital, I suppose," Clodagh replied, pleased to see Ella happy, despite their husbands' obvious disapproval.

"Where are the children?" Ella asked, noticing how quiet the room was.

"With Nanny in the garden. I told them not to stay out too long but the fresh air will do the girls good. There's a farmer's market a few miles inland at the end of the week. I thought the children would enjoy seeing the animals. If you are not busy at the hospital, perhaps we could go?"

"Yes, of course," Ella's eyes danced excitedly. It could be the perfect opportunity to learn something about farming, and if she played her cards right, Fergus may be interested enough to take the idea seriously, having seen for himself a market in action. "I could ask Fergus to come too," she said.

"I think that's a splendid idea, if you can get him away from the mill, that is."

"It's probably not wise for two women in our condition travelling alone with only nanny, Lilly and Mary to accompany us. If I explain it like that, how could he object?"

Clodagh laughed. "Well, quite... how could he?" Clodagh was still unaware of Ella's idea of wanting to start a farm in the countryside outside of Dublin. Ella planned to tell her only if and when she had Fergus firmly on board with the idea. As Fergus had quite rightly said, they didn't want to get anyone's hopes up in case they weren't able to stay.

Workmen had removed saturated carpet from the whole of downstairs, and it was thrown out and piled to the side of the property waiting for collection the next day. They had also dried the floorboards and the musty mildew smell seemed to be fading, thankfully. Molly said goodbye to the last of the workmen and turned to face Ross. "I am shattered." She rubbed her aching brow.

"You've worked hard." Ross took her into his arms and held her tightly.

"So have you," she said wearily over his shoulder.

"How about tomorrow night, me and you, we go tae Eyemouth for dinner, my treat? We've no had a proper chance tae speak and catch up since ye've been back."

He was right, they hadn't had a moment to themselves with all the cleaning after the flood. She still needed to tell him about Adam, and perhaps tomorrow night would be a good opportunity, a chance for her to put the whole Adam saga to bed once and for all. "I'd love to," she replied with a small smile, looking up at him.

"Good, that's settled... I should go. Tell Mrs Winters I'll carry on with the garden tomorrow, now that the house is cleaned up."

"You can call her Daphne, Mrs Winters sounds so formal."

"Yer aunt is formal," he grinned, and Molly giggled.

"Her bark is worse than her bite."

"I'll take yer word for it." He leaned in for a kiss and a moment later he was gone.

Molly wandered into the living room catching Daphne off guard as she sat in the armchair dabbing her eyes with a screwed up handkerchief she'd been nursing. "Auntie, whatever is the matter?"

"Oh Molly don't fuss." Daphne shoved the handkerchief down the side of the armchair.

"I'm not fussing, I'm concerned." Molly perched down on the edge of the sofa nearest to Daphne. "Is it the flood damage, the insurance company are going to pay out, aren't they?"

"Yes, but you heard what that workman said about the wood rot?"

"Not really. There was too much noise behind me with that drying machine."

"He said the wood rot has been in the skirting boards for years and is spreading. He also found it in other places, including the staircase and roof rafters. The insurance company will only pay out for damage caused by the burst pipe, so I'm going to have to foot the bill for the blessed wood rot."

"Gosh, and do you have enough money?"

Daphne sighed heavily and stood up. "I don't know until I get a quote for the whole thing, but that chap's estimated guess was worrying." She walked over to the window and gazed outside with her back turned to Molly so that she wouldn't see her tears welling up again. "I feel like I have bitten off more than I can chew. I'm a silly old fool taking on a project of this size at my time of life. You all warned me, but I didn't listen. There's no fool like an old fool!" She wiped a stray tear away from her cheek.

"You are not a fool, far from it. Together we will sort this. We'll find the money somehow... we've come so far, we can't give up now." Molly got up and selected a log from a pile Ross had brought in earlier.

Daphne blinked through her tears, focusing on the young man walking briskly under the grey stone arch and heading up the path. Had one of the workmen forgotten something? He stopped to admire the entire building, giving an appreciative whistle, and then Daphne suddenly recognised him. "Oh heavens!" she said out loud, without thinking.

"What?" Molly frowned, wiping her hands on her dungarees, having just thrown the log onto the fire.

"Life has just become even more complicated, I'm afraid… more so for you than for me." She turned to face Molly. "You'd better take a look for yourself."

Molly rushed over to the window and gasped in horror.

Chapter Six

Molly opened the door to Adam. "You've got a nerve turning up here like this unannounced. How did you even find me?"

"I had to do some detective work but I got there in the end." A ghost of a smile appeared on his lips. "Can I come in? It's been a long journey."

"Well I can hardly leave you on the doorstep, can I?" She opened the door wider and he walked inside. He gazed up at the high ceiling in awe. "This is an amazing place!"

"Yes, it is," Molly replied coolly, noticing how scruffy and unshaven he looked.

He dragged his attention back to Molly again. "I owe you an apology for standing you up on New Year's Eve."

"You owe her more than an apology, young man; an explanation too, as to why you turned up at Christmas, declaring your undying love for the girl and then didn't show your face until now." Daphne stood with her hands on her hips. "And turning up here without even asking first... Well?"

"I'm sorry... Mrs..." His mind had suddenly gone completely blank; for the life of him, he couldn't remember her name. "My memory fails me again, I do apologise."

"Mrs Winters," she replied sharply. "Your memory seems to fail you a lot, so I hear. Did you forget Molly, your fiancée... forgot that she even existed until now?"

"No I didn't. I've had some trouble at home and I had

no way of contacting her."

"There are such things as telephones," Molly cut in.

"Don't be silly, Molly," Daphne said, facetiously, "it's far easier to jump on a train and go all the way to Scotland.

"I can explain," Adam tried again, his face turning pink from shame.

"Oh take him in the kitchen and make him a cup of tea, for God's sake," Daphne tsked. "I've got far more important things to think about than him!" She tottered off towards the living room again. "And don't let him get off lightly," she called out, not bothering to turn around.

"Come on," Molly led the way to the kitchen.

He placed his large holdall on the floor and sat down at the big wooden table while Molly filled up the kettle and put it on the stove.

"I'm sorry I hurt you, Molly. Trust me when I say it was never my intention."

"Like it was never your intention to tell me you had moved to Portsmouth or that Graham had died?" She turned around to face him.

He looked back at her blankly. "Sorry, I don't follow."

"I went to your house, Adam, on New Year's Eve, after you didn't turn up at the party. An old woman a couple of doors down told me you and your family had moved to Portsmouth after Graham died."

"Graham," he repeated, rapidly trying to think who Graham was.

Molly was quick to pick up on his struggle. "Graham, your brother," she prompted. She was starting to feel guilty for not being more understanding towards his memory loss. It was worse than she had presumed it to be if he didn't even remember his own brother.

"Yes, he uh…"

"It's alright." Molly lifted the kettle off the stove as it

77

began to whistle. "I know this is difficult for you," she said, turning to face him momentarily.

"I... I..." He watched her make the tea, trying to find his words. This was far worse than he had envisaged. She placed the teapot down on the table with two mugs, sugar and milk and poured him a cup of tea. She was about to add a sugar lump when he reached out and stopped her.

"But you've always taken sugar," she said, adding the milk and passing the mug to him.

"Fighting in the trenches, you get used to drinking tea without sugar - sugar was a luxury. In fact, you were lucky if you got a cup of tea at all. And if you did, it was watered down muck, a poor excuse for tea."

"Of course," she smiled sympathetically. "I'm sorry about Graham. But why did you tell me he had broken his arm and he was fine?"

He took a sip of tea and then placed it back down on the table. "The truth is, I didn't remember my parents telling me he had died."

"I see. So why did you tell me he broke his arm?"

"I was confused. I... I was thinking of someone else, someone who reminded me of Graham in my rank... he broke his arm and was sent home. The doctors warned me this could happen, that images and flashbacks can get muddled."

"Did they say if it would improve in time?" Her worried eyes were firmly fixed on his as she brought a mug of tea to her lips.

"They don't know," he replied. "Molly, I know you don't want to be saddled with someone like me, confused all the time, forgetting things. I'm not the man you fell in love with or agreed to marry. Even my own parents can't live with me anymore."

Molly's brow creased into a troubled frown. "What do you mean? They haven't thrown you out, have they?"

He sighed heavily with regret and nodded. "I can't blame them. They found it all too difficult, as do I," he said, blinking away his tears.

"But they can't just cast you aside because you've lost your memory. You served in the war, put your life on the line for your country. You are their son, a war hero. Heavens, does that not mean anything?" She could feel her anger rising before she quickly realised she was actually no better. She was willing to cast him aside, forget about him and move on with Ross. Oh God, Ross. How on earth would she tell him about Adam, and how could she possibly be with him when Adam needed her now more than ever?

"Oh Adam," she reached out and touched his hand. She could see he was in so much emotional torment. "This is all such a mess."

"I know. After our lunch out on Boxing Day, we had such a nice time and you were so lovely, just as you always were, but I couldn't bring myself to see you again, to put you through the pain of seeing me like this. And then... well, things got so bad at home that I didn't know who to turn to, except the only person in the world that I truly love... you." He couldn't control his tears any longer, they streamed down his face like a waterfall of sorrow. Molly left her seat and went to him, placing her arms around his shoulders in comfort, she too could no longer hold back her tears. She had no idea what to do, but she knew she couldn't send him packing, not now, not when he had nowhere to go and was so vulnerable in his current state of mind. He would never have turned his back on her had she become ill, it was only right she stood by him.

The cloudless sky was a glorious deep blue. There was no wind and the temperature was unseasonably warmer than it should have been, making it a perfect day for the McDaniels outing to the farmers' market. Michael was too busy at the mill to come but he was happy for Fergus and Ian to go and do something different. He was all for them enjoying themselves, with any luck it might entice them to stay.

The carriage pulled up at the edge of the field so that the women, both with child, wouldn't have to walk too far. The children jumped down excitedly, and big brother Ian followed behind the little ones as they made their way into the market. It was a good turnout with a variety of animals for sale – pigs, goats, cows, sheep and even ponies. It was busy and noisy as farmers called out their stock for auction and locals gathered around, ready to snatch a bargain or simply watch out of interest.

"That one sounds like you, Lilly!" Ian pointed to one of the pigs and poked his sister playfully.

"And that one *looks* like you," she retorted, giving as good as she got.

Mary giggled, "and that one looks like Uncle Fergus." She pointed to a large pig with floppy ears hanging close to its eyes, resembling Fergus' mop of hair close to his eyes.

The adults were unaware of the conversation, too busy watching the bartering.

Ella turned around to speak to Fergus but he had disappeared.

"Where's Fergus?" Clodagh asked, also noticing that

he was gone.

"That was what I was wondering, some chaperone he turned out to be." Ella smiled, shaking her head.

"There he is," Clodagh pointed over at Fergus talking to a stout, florid looking farmer. "Why's he talking to him? Does he want to buy a cow?" Clodagh said in jest.

It took all Ella's will to hold her tongue, she so much wanted to tell her that they might be interested in running a farm and that he was obviously trying to gain some knowledge from the farmer. Seeing him chat enthusiastically as he was, filled her with hope. "I've no idea," she replied, inwardly excited.

It was late afternoon before they arrived back at Oaklands, having stopped off in a little village en route for lunch. They were in high spirits and the day out had done them all good. The girls ran indoors looking for Nanny, they had so much to tell her and Ian also went with them. Clodagh waddled wearily inside, needing a cup of tea and a sit down. Ella pulled Fergus back for a quiet word. "Just a moment, I want to know what you're thinking. You've been quite chirpy since speaking to that farmer, so come on, tell me?"

"Nothing gets past you, Ella McDaniel," he smiled wryly. "If you must ken, he was very helpful. He gave me a lot of useful information and..." He hesitated, wondering if he should tell her just yet. It still niggled away at the back of his mind that Ireland wasn't far enough from Scotland. But it felt good to be in Dublin and have family around again. If it wasn't necessary to leave for America, why should they throw it all away?

"And what? Come on, don't leave me hanging." Ella stood before him like an excited child, eager to know more.

"He's retiring soon and selling the lease at Tullymore

Farm. He said we could go and take a look. In fact, he's given me first refusal."

"Oh my goodness! Are we going to look? Please say yes…"

"Well there's no harm in looking and I'm keen, I have tae say, but cautious, nonetheless. I'd like tae run it by Michael and get his advice."

"So does that mean I can tell Clodagh?" she asked, beaming from ear to ear.

"Aye, but it's no decided yet and I wouldnae say anything in front of the children. Let's speak about it over dinner this evening."

"Yes, yes of course," she leaned forward and kissed him. "I love you, Fergus McDaniel."

"Dinnae get carried away, we still need tae see the place first. Come on." He placed an arm around her shoulders and they walked up the steps together. He loved to see her so happy. It dawned on him too, that it could be an ideal opportunity to get her away from the hospital. Being on a farm inland, miles from Dublin centre was much safer for her.

The languid flames were struggling to stay alive, so Molly got up and threw a new log on top of the old ones, giving them a poke with a long, iron stoker. It immediately brought warmth back into the living room. Daphne stared at the now roaring fire, preoccupied with her thoughts. Molly resumed her seat on the sofa next to Adam. They had all consumed the homemade shepherd's pie that Mrs Brady, the cook, had prepared earlier that day and left out for them to warm up. Adam glanced over at Daphne. Conversation over dinner had been minimal and he knew if he was to stay, he needed to break the ice with her somehow. "Mrs Winters," he said, this time remembering her name. "I would like to thank you for allowing me to stay and I'm very sorry I didn't ask first before arriving."

Molly smiled proudly, pleased that he was making an effort.

"It's not me you need to thank, it's Molly. She's far more forgiving than I would have been, but you're here now so you'd best make yourself useful around the place."

"Oh, I will," he replied enthusiastically. "Would you still like to have the outbuildings turned into stables?"

"I would, but the only payment you'll get is your board and keep," she replied, giving him a stern look. It was no secret that she wasn't impressed with the lad but she resisted making a complete judgement on the account of his head injury. For that reason alone, she had agreed he could stay.

"Auntie has to save her money for the wood rot repairs," Molly said, feeling the need to explain.

"Wood rot? Every carpenter's worst nightmare, but I know how to treat it."

"You do?" both Molly and Daphne replied in unison.

"Yes of course," he smirked, looking at their surprised faces. "I'd not be much of a carpenter if I didn't. Where is the rot?"

"The skirting boards in the hallway, in some of the rooms upstairs and in the roof rafters too, so I'm told," Daphne said with a sigh. "I think it'll be too big a job for one man," she added, wishing of course, that it wasn't. It would save her an enormous amount of money if she didn't have to pay a company to sort it and she wasn't even sure she could afford it.

"You'd be surprised. I'm a quick worker."

"But are you a good worker? I don't want some rushed, cowboy job." She narrowed her eyes at him.

"Auntie!" Molly chided. "Adam is a professional. He did his apprenticeship at Portsmouth dockyard."

Daphne harrumphed. "I don't need him to build me a sodding boat!"

"Wood, is wood, whether it be in a house or a boat, Mrs Winters. It's always susceptible to rot - even more so on a boat due to damp conditions."

"So, you are saying you know what you are doing?" she challenged.

"Yes, I do."

Adam was up early the next morning. Before breakfast, he had already checked out the wood rot all over the house and was now aware of the size of the job. He was prepared to tackle it alone, he had a fair idea of how to treat it, and felt it his duty to at least try. After all, he was receiving free board for his services and, if he wanted to be with Molly, he'd have no choice but to knuckle down and do his best. If he did manage to sort the problem, it would certainly work in his favour if it saved old Mrs Winters a small fortune, and she could then afford to pay him for the outbuilding conversions.

Daphne decided to stay in bed a little longer this morning. Her hip had been playing up and the stress of the flood and the discovery of the wood rot had taken its toll on her; she was tired and needed to rest. And she was not the only one who felt tired. Molly had tossed and turned practically all night, not knowing what to do about the situation she now found herself in. Just thinking about ending her relationship with Ross brought her to tears, and telling Adam the truth and letting him go made her feel guilty, like she had betrayed him in the worst possible way. She was relieved that Daphne had told Adam he was to sleep in the west wing on the other side of the house, as far away as possible from Molly. Daphne had strict morals, especially when it came to unbridled sex, not that Molly would have broken that rule, of course. She had agreed with Adam to wait until they were married and now more than ever, she was glad they had made that pact.

"I'll need to go to the nearest town to buy a product for the rot," Adam said, accepting a plate of scrambled eggs on toast from Molly. She then poured him a cup of tea.

"Eyemouth is the nearest town. We have a truck in the garage. Are you allowed to drive in your condition?"

"My condition?" he chuckled, tucking hungrily into his breakfast.

"You know what I mean… your memory problem."

"Are you afraid I'll lose the truck, forget where I parked it, is that it? You can come with me to make sure I don't." He looked up at her and smiled half-heartedly, noticing how pale and tired she was compared to yesterday.

A knock on the back door made Molly jump - she was a bag of nerves. The door opened and Ross wandered in, much to her dismay. "Morning, ma bonnie princess!" he said, wearing a bright smile. "I've just left a pile of chopped firewood on the back porch for you." He planted a kiss on her cheek.

Molly could feel the colour rising in her face. Adam gave Ross the once over from head to toe with both distaste and confusion. "Thank you," she replied, trying to conceal her embarrassment in front of Adam.

"I'm looking forward tae this evening. You Miss Molly are going tae be spoilt rotten, and you deserve tae be." He then noticed Adam with quizzical eyes, having been oblivious to him so far. "Sorry we havenae met, have we? I'm Ross McDaniel." He held out his hand across the table in a friendly gesture, presuming he was probably a workman of some sort, hired by Daphne.

Adam stood up abruptly, causing his chair to fall away with a loud clatter behind him, his short fuse was getting the better of him. "Get away from my fiancée." He leaned over the table. She's mine! You better watch yourself!"

"Fiancée? You're Adam?"

"Yes, I'm Adam, back from the dead," he replied disdainfully. "And I'm going to punch you into next week if I ever hear you talking to my girl like that again.

Ross looked back at Molly, perplexed.

"Ross, I'm sorry, I was going to tell you this morning and then…" Before she could finish her sentence, he had fled out of the back door. She ran into the garden, calling after him but he was too upset to stop and listen. She decided to give him some space. Furious with Adam for his outburst of anger, she went back inside. "You had no right to say that to Ross. I am not yours!" she shouted.

"Well I'm sorry but I beg to differ. When I put a ring on your finger you became promised to me, so you are as good as mine." He looked down at her left hand. "I notice you don't bother to wear my ring these days… why not? Where is it?"

"At Hazleton Farm. I took it off when I thought you were never coming back. When I thought it was time to move on because you were… you were dead." She wiped her tears rapidly away with the palms of her hands.

"Dead! Yes, how convenient that would have been, me dead. You could move on with your life, with your fancy man. You didn't let the grass grow, did you? It all makes sense now, why you were so hesitant for us to be together when I returned, why you needed time to think about *us*."

"What? You've no idea what I've been through. It was hell for me every day, wishing, praying and hoping for your safety and for you to come back home. I grieved for you for months on end, locked in my bedroom crying day after day, night after night."

"Oh, boohoo! You had it really tough, poor, little Molly sitting in your cosy ivory tower with your cosy little family, while I was out there getting blown to bits!"

She shook her head, tears streaming down her face. "I don't know who you are any more. The Adam I fell in love with would never have spoken to me like this."

"That's because the Adam you fell in love with *is* dead!"

"What do you mean?" She stared back at him through clouded eyes.

Adam exhaled deeply, calming his nerves, getting a grip of himself. "A part of me died out there in France," he said in a sombre tone. "I'm doing my best, Molly. I just need your support."

"I need some air and don't follow me," she said, unable to bear him any longer.

He sat back down, burying his head in his large weatherbeaten hands. He hoped he had not just screwed things up and she wasn't going to come back and throw him out.

Molly grabbed her coat and ran out of the front door, down the steps and across the courtyard. Ross threw down the spade in his hand and ran after her. By the time he had caught up with her, she was already entering the field opposite Aberdoch Manor. "Is that it now? Adam is back so it's over between us?" He tugged on her arm forcing her to stop and face him.

"What do you expect me to say, Ross?" She was crying openly.

"I expect you tae tell me the truth. Tell me if you love *him* or me."

"It's not that simple, it's far from simple," she cried. "He has been through hell and back, he's had major surgery to his brain, and face and he's lost his memory, his own family have turned their back on him. I'm all he's got." She started walking away again and Ross quickened his pace to match hers.

"I'm sorry, especially about his family. I know only too well what he's gone through, I was there too, fighting for king and country, but you should not be forced tae be with him out of pity, Molly."

"Who said it was pity?" She glanced at him sideways through her tears. "I agreed to marry him, I love him."

"Do you?" He stopped her again. "Tell me that again. Look me in the eyes and tell me you love Adam and you don't love me. And I promise I'll respect your decision and leave you alone, even if it kills me tae do so."

She shook her head - she couldn't. It was impossible to tell him she didn't love him, because it was not true. She loved him with all her heart, which only made the situation harder. She ran as fast as she could, straight for the Ghost Tree up ahead. She needed to escape - escape both Adam and Ross, go back to her old life - a life where she loved only one man – Fergus McDaniel. Ross could see that was where she was heading and sprinted after her. "Molly, ye know ye cannae touch the Ghost Tree!" His words fell on deaf ears. "It's dangerous, Molly... don't do it!"

She ran up to the tree and with her hand held out. Ross stumbled over the huge roots of the ancient yew tree poking out above the surrounding grass. And as he raced to stop her, both their hands fell hopelessly onto the inscribed heart. They instantly fell to the ground, their bodies limp staring wildly in a vacant trance. It only took seconds for the darkness to follow, as their minds travelled back - beyond birth, beyond death and back to their previous lives.

Chapter Seven

"Tullymore Farm? Aye, old Mr Doyle owns it. Ma Pa kent him years ago when he worked down at the harbour on the boats. He must have had that farm near on twenty years now," said Michael. "So he's retiring, is he?"

"Aye, and we're thinking about taking over the lease," Fergus announced, gazing across the table at Ella's happy face.

"Really? Are you really going to stay?" Clodagh piped up, clapping her hands together gleefully.

Ella nodded and Clodagh reached out and hugged her.

"We think we'd like tae make Ireland our home, aye," Fergus confirmed.

"Cousin, you never cease to amaze me. A farmer, well, well, well." Michael beamed. "Tae have you all living nearby is going to be wonderful, isn't it Clodagh?"

"Absolutely! Mary will be thrilled not to have to say goodbye to Lilly."

"Mary will be able to come and see the animals whenever she likes. Ella patted a hand gently on Clodagh's belly, "and the little one, when it arrives."

"We've no told the children yet, and I prefer if it wasnae mentioned until we've seen it and ken for sure," said Fergus. "We dinnae want tae get their hopes up too soon."

"I'll certainly miss you and young Ian at the mill," Michael said thoughtfully. "But it's a small price tae pay for you no setting off into the sunset. Do you have any knowledge of farming?"

"Fergus gave a short laugh. "Not the first thing, but

I'm a fast learner, it cannae be that difficult."

"Dinnae let old Doyle hear ye say that, I'm sure he'd argue otherwise," Michael grinned, wryly. "I ken a man who was a farmer for a number of years, I can send him yer way to give you some advice and such like."

"Thanks, Michael, it could be helpful." Michael raised his glass. "To the McDaniels, may we have a long, healthy and prosperous life together in Ireland – Slàinte Mhath!"

"Slàinte Mhath!" they repeated in chorus, raising their wine glasses in the air.

Ella had not felt this happy for a long time as she sat on the edge of the bed while Fergus unfastened the back of her gown. As it dropped from her shoulders, he kissed her bare neck, sending tingles of excitement through her body. "Fergus," Ella whispered breathlessly, "do you feel sure we are doing the right thing?"

He suddenly stopped kissing her and swung his legs to sit by her side, wearing nothing more than a long, cotton shirt. His coppery brows pressed together. "About the farm?"

"About the farm, yes." She just needed to hear him say they were.

"Aye, well, there'll be a lot tae learn and tae do, running a farm, I dinnae doubt that," he admitted. "But with young Ian helping out too, and Lilly will when she gets older, I think we'll manage."

"And being in Ireland, are we going to be safe here?" she asked, with concern. Memories of the Red Coats after her still haunted her at times.

He thought for a moment, contemplating his answer carefully. Of course he could not be certain about their safety, but he had a good feeling about being in Dublin, and moving further inland into the countryside was a wise plan.

"I think if the Red Coats thought we were in Dublin, they'd have been here by now. As Michael says, the Red Coats will only keep searching in England and Scotland until they get tired of looking. And as for the McKenzies, they got what they wanted, they killed... he took a deep breath, controlling his emotions... they killed those we cared about most and those we loved, and they drove us out of our home, they have achieved what they wanted." His jaw set in a firm line. His anger always brewed every time he thought about the McKenzies and what they did.

"I love you." She smothered his right cheek with plentiful kisses.

"Oh aye, how much?" he teased, pulling her dress away from her and laying her back on the bed in just her underwear, which he began slowly peeling off bit by bit, revealing her perfectly formed baby bump. "I'll be gentle," he whispered in her ear, lifting his shirt up and lowering himself carefully, entering her slowly and tenderly." She groaned from each gentle move back and forth, until they became one with each other, lost in a climax of ecstasy.

They both sat beneath the yew tree, looking dazed while they came to their senses. "My God!" Ross spoke first, staring directly at Molly. "I... I..." He was lost for words.

"What did you see, Ross?" She was still trying to bring herself back to the here and now. A moment ago she had been in another world, making love with her husband, Fergus. And now she was back in 1946 again, sitting next to Ross. He looked so bewildered and as confused as she was. "What did you see?" she repeated.

"Myself, with Ella," he replied, the images on them in bed were still very vivid in his mind.

"With me?" She raised her brow with surprise. "You saw Ella?"

"Yes, Ella. We were… my God, we were..." He held her questioning stare for a moment, trying to find the right words. "We were in bed, together… you were pregnant."

She jumped up in utter shock, realisation now sweeping over her. Ross was Fergus, it was all so much clearer now. That was why he reminded her of Fergus so much. "You're… you were Fergus?" Her voice was nothing more than a soft whisper but he heard her, all the same.

"Yes. All this time I thought Fergus McDaniel was my ancestor, but he wasn't, I was Fergus," he said with absolute certainty.

"But what if…" Her mind was racing, exploring different options. "What if you didn't see yourself but you saw your ancestor, Fergus? This tree," she pointed to the ancient yew tree, "it's called the Ghost Tree, we are meant to see ghosts, aren't we?"

Ross stood up. "Ghosts of the past, aye, and in this situation, our own ghosts, reflections of time. I cannae believe you just asked me that."

"You doubted me enough times when I told you I was Ella, you didn't believe me. In fact, I was beginning to think you would never believe me," she said with a weary sigh.

"Well I do believe you, especially now… Molly, do you remember you said you could see yourself, hear your own thoughts, feel everything, sense everything as real as you are doing right now?"

"Yes, that is exactly it."

"Precisely, and that's what happened tae me. I was Fergus, I could feel his emotions, know what he was feeling because they were my own thoughts, my own feelings." He took Molly's hands into his own. "We were deeply in love, married, no less." He was awash with emotion. "You were having ma baby. And we had more..." he frowned, remembering their names. "Lilly and Ian?"

"They were not ours," Molly corrected him. "They were your sister's children. Shona died during the night of the McKenzie massacre."

He screwed up his face in horror. "God, really?"

"She was trying to escape Aberdoch Manor and fell down the stairs to her death. We managed to rescue the children, Lilly and Ian, and we fled to safety."

"Did you see it happen, when you touched the tree before?" He hoped she hadn't, for her sake.

She shook her head. "No, don't you remember? You stopped me from touching the tree when I discovered about the massacre. But I had flashbacks when Henry, my brother told me of his research into Aberdoch Manor.

"Aye, I remember now. How could I forget? It was the first time we kissed." He remembered how distressed she had been running towards the tree, wanting to go back in time to stop the massacre. But Ross had reminded her that when she went back, she had no recollection of her present life, so there was no way that she could change what was about to happen. She had been devastated to learn this, and he had calmed her down and they had kissed for the very first time.

"Ross, we should get back," she glanced at her watch, they had been gone for almost two and a half hours. "Auntie will be getting worried."

"Aye, of course, but Molly, before we go." He glided the back of his hand gently down the side of her face. "You must see we've been brought together in this life again for a reason." He pointed at the inscribed heart with the initials E&F. "That heart symbolises our love, our unbreakable bond. What we just shared, seeing each other in our last lives, is every proof that we are destined to be together. Please tell me you can see that."

She knew he was right, and looking at him standing before her, all she could see was Fergus again, just as she had the first time he had kissed her. He was her true love, a love that lived on for an eternity. She nodded. He wiped away a stray tear from her cheek. "You're going tae have tae face Adam and tell him."

"I can't tell him any of this, he would never believe me." She took Ross' hand as they began to walk back through the field. "Give me some time to sort it. Please stay away from the house so as not to antagonise him."

"Antagonise him? Molly, it kills me tae think he's flirting with you, touching you, kissing you…"

"No, Ross, he's not doing any of those things and I wouldn't let him if he tried. I must do this my way and if you love me, you'll give me the space I need."

Ross returned to his gardening, still shell shocked about his discovery - that he had lived a previous life and not just any life, but he had been Fergus McDaniel. Everything he had researched in the past wasn't about his ancestor, it had been about himself. He was Laird McDaniel, the leader of clan McDaniel, a Jacobite warrior, fighting for what he believed in. The very idea seemed inconceivable but it was as true as he was standing there right now as Ross McDaniel living a life in 1946. It was all so surreal, especially to think that he had come back as a McDaniel again, born into the same family. But the biggest astonishment of all was how Molly had come all the way from the south of England to live in Aberdoch Manor, their home from two hundred years ago. How their paths had come to cross again, fate bringing them together once more - his wife from 1746! Overcome with emotion, he stood for a moment trying to absorb it all.

"Where have you been all this time?" Daphne placed a cup of tea down on the coffee table before lowering herself gently into the armchair. Her hip was still aching even after her lie in that morning.

"Morning walk to clear my head," Molly said, entering the living room. The sunlight was pouring in through the window and highlighting a film of dust over the coffee table. Daphne spotted it too, and gave a loud tsk, wiping her finger through it. "I'll need to get that maid starting work soon, I just didn't want to pay out wages until we were up and running."

"I can do the dusting," Molly said, flopping down on the sofa. "Where's Adam?" she asked cautiously.

"Gone to Eyemouth to get a product for the wood rot." She narrowed her eyes at Molly. "Did you two have a barney this morning? I heard raised voices when I was trying to sleep."

"Sorry, yes, we had words."

"Enough words to fill a bloomin' dictionary by the sounds of it. What happened?" Daphne frowned, watching Molly closely.

"Ross came into the kitchen and Adam didn't like it. And he said some things he shouldn't have."

"Who? Ross or Adam?"

Adam. Ross wasn't to blame - he had no idea who Adam was."

"And whose fault is that? I told you that you needed to

sit down and tell them both what's what."

"I know, Auntie, but it all happened so quickly, what with the flood and then Adam turning up out of the blue like that."

"Well, it's done now. I suppose Ross is heartbroken. Shame, I was starting to quite like him," Daphne mumbled, pensively

"Really? I didn't think you liked anyone."

"Of course I do. Well, not many… most people have a habit of irritating me like that damn vicar and his wife."

"Vicar Norman was very helpful with the flood," Molly reminded her. "and Joan is a kind person - she means well."

"You're going off topic. How did Ross take the news?"

"It's complicated," Molly sighed.

"What's complicated? Your fiancé is back and that's that. You can't carry on with two men at the same time," she scoffed.

"And I don't intend to, but I don't feel the same way about Adam as I used to."

Daphne wriggled in her chair to try and get more comfortable. "You need to think things through carefully, no rash decisions."

"What do you mean?"

"Well, he's got nowhere to go, so he says. And he's starting to sort out the wood rot."

Suddenly realisation dawned on Molly. "That's why you don't want me to send him packing, because of the wood rot."

"Molly, you make me sound shallow," she said pursing her lips. "But he could save this place. The cost of restoring the wood rot is more than I can afford."

"How do you know for sure?" Molly asked, grabbing the cushion next to her and resting her chin on the top of it.

"That chap I spoke to, he called back this morning when you were out. I nearly dropped the phone when he gave me the estimate."

"I see. Well we could always get another estimate, they are not the only company, I'm sure."

"Or we could just let Adam do the job. I'll pay him for it, enough to see him alright and then he can be on his way with money in his pocket. If you don't send him packing just yet, that is."

"So you are asking me to carry on with this false pretence? Let him think that we are going to get married and live happily ever after? And what am I supposed to tell Ross in the meantime?"

"Molly, listen to me." Daphne looked at her squarely. "This hotel is going to be all yours one day. This is your future we are talking about here. If I can't pay for the wood rot to be treated, and have to walk away from this place, you can say goodbye to running your own hotel and you will go back to working at Hazleton Farm. Is that what you want?"

"No, of course not but…"

"But nothing, Molly. It's plain and simple. You keep Adam sweet, then when he finishes the work, I pay him and you can wish him a nice life and start yours again. And Ross will just have to be patient."

As Ella entered Mercer's hospital, she was greeted by a scene she was unprepared for. There were more patients than beds, the sick had resorted to lying on the cold stone floors, many with high fevers and vomiting. The stench hit her the moment she had stepped inside the building. Amelia, having spotted Ella at the entrance, came racing towards her with a dirty bed pan in hand. "It's smallpox," she announced with a face the colour of crimson. "Have you had it?"

"Yes, when I was a child." Ella immediately understood her reason for asking.

"Thank the Lord!" Can you take care of them up the far end. I've had no chance yet, I've been dealing with these new ones just in.

"Of course," Ella removed her cape in haste. "Amelia," she said, looking back over her shoulder. "Have you had it too?"

"Yes, thankfully, so we are both safe." She dashed off to empty the bed pan, leaving Ella to get stuck in with her work.

Ross turned around at the sound of crunching tyres as the old brown truck, driven by Adam, arrived under the stone arch and made its way to the garage. A moment later, Adam crossed the courtyard holding a large container of some kind of liquid and went indoors. Ross stood for a moment, watching the front door close. He envied how Adam could just wander into the house and be close to Molly, be able to speak with her whenever he wanted, and dine with her. Dine? Oh goodness he needed to cancel the reservation at that swanky restaurant he had booked in Eyemouth for this evening. He had saved his money to take Molly somewhere special and had been looking forward to it, just the two of them spending time alone, no Mrs Winters hanging around. But instead Molly would be with him – Adam.

It was half past four when Ross put the gardening tools away in the shed and made his way through the courtyard and into the fields. He always walked across the fields to go home; it was much shorter than going down the lane and then walking along the main road. Lost in thought as he had been all day, he suddenly noticed he was approaching the Ghost Tree. He stopped and gazed up at it. He had walked past that tree for years and although he knew its name the Ghost Tree was given for a reason, now he saw the tree with different eyes. The inscribed heart on the thick and twisted bark, he realised had to have been carved by himself, when he had lived as Fergus. Its huge frame of evergreen needle-like leaves stood towering above him. If only trees could speak, he mused. He then pondered what would happen if he were to touch the heart again while being alone. It had worked for Molly when she had been alone, more than once, but when he had touched it before, years ago, he had not seen his past life but had seen his late mother instead. Why had he not seen himself then, he wondered. Perhaps it was Molly coming into his life again that had made this happen. Perhaps her presence, her being in Aberdoch was enough to spark this magical power of being able to see his past life. If he would touch the tree right now, would it happen again? Would he see himself, Fergus McDaniel? He possessed a burning desire to know more about his past life. What had his life been like back then? Although he didn't know what year it had been when he and Molly went back in time, he knew from his research about Fergus, it must have been around the mid to late 1700s.

He brought his hand to the inscribed heart and it hovered there for a moment as he contemplated the outcome - should he touch it again? Then, not being able to resist and throwing caution to the wind, he pressed his palm firmly down on the rough bark.

Fergus entered the drawing room and found Clodagh sitting alone by the fire. Nanny had just taken the children upstairs and Ian had followed too.

"Where's Ella?" Fergus asked, reaching for the whisky decanter placed on a highly polished table. He poured himself a glass, took a swig and faced Clodagh expectantly for her reply.

Clodagh was uncomfortable with his question. She was well aware of how Fergus felt about Ella spending time at the hospital. "I'm afraid she's not back yet."

"She's no back from the hospital?" Fergus frowned with deep concern.

Clodagh shook her head with regret.

"She shouldnae be walking the streets of Dublin alone in the dark," Michael remarked, walking into the room having overheard the tail end of their conversation.

Fergus downed the whisky and placed his glass back down on the table. "I must search for her at once."

"I will come with ye, I'll have Alfred prepare a horse and carriage." Michael left the room in haste.

As the carriage made its way down the lane away from Oaklands, Fergus felt sick from worry. Ella could have run into any number of dangerous situations, including, God forbid, the Red Coats discovering where she was. Just the thought of that made him shudder. He would never forgive himself if anything had happened to her. Her safety had always come first, as did Lilly's and Ian's. He regretted ever agreeing to her helping out at the hospital - she needed to be at Oaklands with Clodagh, where he knew she was safe.

There was a mist rolling in again from the harbour as they made their way into the village of Tallaght. And heading towards them on the opposite side of the road, like an apparition, a carriage appeared through the mist. Fergus shouted out for the driver to stop, forcing the carriage to a halt. He had a hunch Ella could be on board. There wouldn't be many travelling in the direction of Oaklands at this time of night. And his hunch served him right. Ella poked her head out of the tiny window to see why they had suddenly come to a standstill. Realising it was Fergus standing at the carriage door, she immediately opened it and stepped out, grabbing hold of his hand as he guided her down safely. He suddenly hugged her tightly from relief, and it came clear to her from his embrace that he had been immensely worried. "I'm sorry," she said, looking up at him apologetically. "I was needed at the hospital and the time escaped me."

"I'll pay for your carriage," he said, sternly. "Now get inside." His relief had turned to anger as he ushered her in the direction of Michael waiting with the carriage door open for her.

"Ella." Michael greeted her with a small courteous smile as he helped her into the carriage.

A moment later they turned around and were on their way back to Oaklands. Fergus held his tongue, not wishing to discuss the matter in front of Michael. Ella sat quietly, knowing better than to try and explain further on their journey back, there would be plenty of time for that when they were alone in their room.

When they arrived at Oaklands, Ella rushed indoors.

Without entering the drawing room to say hello to Clodagh, she ran upstairs to their bedroom, ready for the battle she knew awaited her. A moment later, Fergus entered the bedroom.

"Before you say anything," she said, perched on the end of the bed, looking exhausted and really not having the strength to fight with him, "there was an outbreak of smallpox, I had to help."

"Smallpox?" Fergus stared back at her aghast. "And you stayed there knowing how infectious smallpox is?"

"It's not infectious to me, I had it as a small child, you can only get it once in a lifetime."

He appeared momentarily relieved. "That aside, look at you Ella, ye're exhausted, worn out."

"I'll be fine, I just need to sleep." She arched her back against the dull ache both in her shoulders and lower back.

"You are no tae go back there, do ye hear me?" he stood before her, his eyes pouring into hers. "I mean it."

"We agreed six weeks, I've only been there two and they need me now more than ever," she replied in her defence.

"I don't care," he retorted raising his voice. "I am your husband. I make the rules!"

"Rules that are unjust." She glared back at him. "I am able to help the sick, I cannot put myself in any danger so I really don't think…"

"Every time ye go there, ye put yourself in danger," his voice was still raised. "I am worried sick about you and our unborn bairn… every time ye leave this house and venture into Dublin. I willnae permit it any longer. It is ma duty as your husband and head of this family tae protect you, whether you like it or no. If I find out you've gone tae that place again, there'll be serious consequences," he said, making his point clear, "and ye can forget about the farm, because I willnae stay here a minute longer with you and the children. We will be on the first boat out of here tae America. Do ye hear me, Ella?"

Her tears trickled softly down both cheeks as she nodded, having no choice but to agree with him.

He hated to make her cry, but it was for her own good and the good of their unborn child. "Do I have your word, you willnae return tae the hospital, not ever?" He held her stare, challengingly.

She took a deep breath and exhaled, wiping the tears from her face. "I…" She struggled to answer him. Agreeing to not go back to the hospital felt like a betrayal to Amelia and those who desperately needed her right now, but if she was to go against his wishes, that would be a betrayal to her husband, to his trust, to their family, and furthermore prevent their future happiness of putting down roots and running a farm in Ireland.

"Ella? Do I have your word?" he pressed eagerly and with determination.

Ross' eyelids fluttered and then slowly opened. It was now dark, all bar the moon casting a soft silver glow on himself and the Ghost Tree behind him. His mouth felt dry and his head was pounding as he raised to his feet. He walked away from the tree, making his way across the field home, reliving the images in his mind. Fergus and Ella had been in Dublin, so that was where they must have escaped to after the Aberdoch Massacre, which made perfect sense as to why Eyemouth library had run dry on information past that time. He felt like he had been hit by a truck as he stumbled a little trying to gain his balance and understand everything he had just witnessed. The fear and worry he carried for Ella's safety and his unborn child was paramount. He realised he loved her so very dearly. A love that ran incredibly deep was continuing now in his new life, in both their new lives. Their bodies had died previously but their love for each other still lived on.

Chapter Eight

"I'm making a cuppa if you want one?" Molly passed Adam on the stairs. He was carrying a dust sheet up to the landing to start work on the skirting boards.

"I never say no to a cuppa, especially when a pretty girl is offering to make me one." He flashed a cheeky grin, which Molly preferred to ignore. She headed off to the kitchen without another word.

Mrs Brady had just left and there was a scrumptious aroma of homemade bread from the loaf cooling on the worktop. Molly peered inside of a large pot on the stove, Mrs Brady had also made stew for their supper. She inhaled it, looking forward to eating it later. She picked up the kettle and walked over to the sink and almost dropped it from fright as Adam placed his arms unexpectedly around her waist. "What are you doing?" She spun around and glared at him. "Get your hands off me."

"Mol," he frowned, baffled at her reaction to him showing her any kind of affection. "We are engaged," he reminded her. "Not that anyone would guess. Honestly, you're as cold as the morning frost."

"You... you took me by surprise and I didn't like it." She placed the kettle down and lit the stove.

"So I can see. Would you like me to give you a ten minute warning next time before approaching? Maybe an air raid siren should do the job." He sat down at the table with a weary sigh.

"You've changed, you know. You've become very

sarcastic." Molly stood with her arms folded, looking at him.

"Yes, well, war does that to you. Funny that, hey!" His tone was bitter.

She sat down at the table and, softening his approach again, he reached out for her hand. "Come on Molly, I'm doing my best, meet me half way at least."

"If that's your best, hurling insults at me, calling me cold as frost, I'd hate to see your worst." She pulled her hand abruptly away from his.

"I'm sorry but you are really distant towards me. We had some good times in the past, didn't we? We can't forget them."

She relented with a small smile, feeling guilty. "Yes… yes, we did." Her smile grew. "I remember when you took me to meet your family for the first time. You were so nervous." She chuckled. "I will never forget your grandma. Do you remember when I met her? Her false teeth…" she prompted, waiting for some kind of recognition. But it was clear he had no clue what she was talking about.

"Yes, Grandma had false teeth." He forced a smile, trying to go along with the story. It was tiring to keep saying he didn't remember.

"When your mother handed us all a homemade scone and Grandma took a bite, her teeth fell out onto her plate." Molly gave a short snoot of laughter. "Then she sat forward and they accidently fell on the floor and her dog, you know the cute little Scottie, can't remember his name now, but he gave her teeth a good old lick. "Your face was a picture, you turned as red as a tomato."

"Well I suppose it wouldn't have been the best way to impress a girl," Adam said, feeling agitated again.

"You don't remember, do you?" she asked sorrowfully.

"No, I'm afraid I don't and I wish you wouldn't keep looking at me that way."

"What way?" The kettle whistled and Molly got up to make the tea.

"Like you pity me."

"I don't pity you; I pity the situation, but not you."

"The situation? Me being here?"

Molly didn't reply as she busied around the kitchen. He found himself staring at her back as she reached for the tea-cups, standing on her tip toes. He knew she wasn't thrilled at him being there at Aberdoch Manor, but he didn't understand why. He also knew he needed to work harder if he had any chance of staying with her indefinitely.

"There is something I remember well. I remember you sending me a letter with a scented pink ribbon from your hair and a photograph of yourself sitting on a bright red tractor. God, you looked sexy."

"Oh, Adam," she blushed. "At least you remember that." She watched him carefully. It must be awful living without a memory; no memories to cherish from the past. She couldn't imagine how difficult it must be for him.

"I remember you said in your letters that you'd been helping your dad make homemade wine and it had turned out disastrously - it exploded or something?"

"Oh yes, it did and we got covered from head to toe in this sticky, stinking substance that he called wine. It neither looked nor smelt anything like it," she giggled, remembering her father's face covered in the messy liquid.

"And in one of your letters, your mum had made a Victoria sandwich cake for the church fair and the dog ate it." He sighed wistfully. "Your letters made me laugh, kept my spirits high when I needed it most."

"I can't believe you remembered my letters," she

smiled broadly, then grew pensive. "How strange that you remember them, but not other things."

"What are you insinuating?" He bristled at her comment, picking up his cup of tea.

"Nothing, I'm just saying it's funny how you remember my letters but not other things." It was happening again. One minute he was fine and the next he was so defensive. She felt like she was forever walking on eggshells.

"Funny? I'd hardly call it funny. Is that not enough for now, that I remember your letters? Perhaps it's just because I read them so many times, that's why I remember them well."

"Of course," she smiled softly. "How are you getting on with treating the wood rot?" she asked, changing the subject. It seemed easier to talk about the present rather than the past, or maybe not.

"Fine, why do you ask?"

"Just interested, no other reason."

"Interested in wood rot?" He placed the tea-cup down on the table without drinking. "You need to get out more if that's your entertainment round here, wondering about wood rot."

"I wonder about it because it is destroying my business, my future hotel."

"*Your* future hotel? That sounds very much like we aren't a team. I thought marriage was about sharing. Do you not think I want to protect our future too?"

"We're not married yet. If I may say so, you are being a tad presumptuous," she retorted, standing up and pouring the remainder of her cup of tea down the sink. He was grating on her nerves and she needed to leave the room before she said something she might regret.

"Presumptuous? Seems to me our engagement means nothing to you, maybe you have no intention of marrying me at all."

"I...I," she couldn't find her words. Flustered, she walked towards the door.

He jumped off his chair and reached for her arm, pulling her back abruptly. "Cat got your tongue?" He spat his words with both anger and frustration. "You frigid cow!" The fear was apparent in her eyes and he realised he had gone too far and should back down before it was too late. "I'm sorry, I didn't mean to scare you. I just get so wound up. I want to move on but I can't plan a future with you because you just don't seem committed - it's like you don't want what we have anymore." He released his grip and she broke free, rubbing her arm against the sting on her skin.

"That's because I don't know what we have anymore. It's all changed. You've changed."

"So you keep saying, but maybe you have changed too. Maybe you are not as perfect as you think you are."

"I don't think I'm perfect," Molly replied sharply. "But yes, you're right, maybe I have changed too." She knew full well she had, she was in love with Ross and it hurt to be apart from him and she was already starting to resent Adam for it, although she knew it was not entirely his fault.

"And there we have it, at last some honesty."

Molly stared back at him incredulously. "You always want to belittle me, don't you? I know that you are not well Adam, but you must try to understand this is difficult for me, too."

"Not half as difficult as it is for me," he mumbled, brushing past her. "I've got work to be done. We'll pick up with this conversation later."

"Great, I can't wait!" Molly mocked, watching him walk away, wondering how much more of him she could take.

Daphne placed the receiver back down from the phone and entered the living room, feeling worried. She walked over to the window and stood for a moment, pensive, as she gazed out onto the extensive gardens. Her eyes focused momentarily on Ross busy trimming a hedge in the distance.

"Auntie," Molly broke Daphne's troubled thoughts. She turned around, the worry still very much displayed all over her face.

"What's wrong?" Molly asked, realising immediately something was bothering her.

"I hope to God Adam can fix the wood rot. Acting on your advice to get another quote, I just received one from a different company, and it was more than the first one."

"How much more?" Molly frowned.

"See for yourself, there's the notepad." She pointed at it on the coffee table.

Molly read it then looked back at Daphne with a look of horror. "That's extortionate. "How much money from the cheaper quote do you have?"

"Why? Don't you think Adam is up to the job?"

"Honestly, I don't know."

"I've got about half that money, so he better be."

"Right," Molly ripped out the page and flung the notepad back down on the table. "I'm nipping out," she said. "I won't be long."

"Where to? The new linen is arriving soon, I wanted you to help me with it." Daphne's words fell on deaf ears, Molly was already grabbing her coat and making her way out of the front door. She ran across the courtyard and entered the field. The sun was poking through intermittently between grey clouds after a recent downpour. In the distance, a rainbow was forming over the small hamlet of Aberdoch.

She stopped for a moment at the Ghost Tree, glancing up at its branches dripping drops of rain water. She smiled meekly, thinking of Fergus, which in turn led her to think of Ross. It still felt so surreal to think that Fergus was now Ross. A pang of heartache spurred her on in her mission to help Aunt Daphne. If she could raise the other half of the money, she could sit down with Adam properly and explain about Ross. She would let Adam stay at Aberdoch Manor for a while if he wanted. He could even fix up the stables as originally planned, instead of the wood rot, earn some money and then be on his way. At least she wouldn't have to live a lie any more. It could all be out in the open. Adam was no longer the same person and Molly knew in her heart she would resent him for the rest of her life if she married him. Her future was with Ross and she had never felt more certain than she did right now. Her decision was final.

"Good timing, love, I was just making a cuppa," Joan said as Norman hung up his coat. "I've only just got in myself."

"How did your walk go?" Norman asked, taking off his shoes.

"Good. We did a seven mile hike, my feet are dropping off."

"Well, I'm very proud of you." He planted a kiss on her cheek, having followed her into the kitchen.

"And how was your day?" She placed the kettle on the stove.

"Good. Mrs Jones popped into the church about her grandson's christening just as I was…"

The loud knock on the door stopped Norman in mid flow. "I'll get it," he said, forcing himself off the chair where he had just sat down.

"Molly, what a lovely surprise." Norman smiled. He

beckoned her inside.

"I hope I'm not intruding, it's just I needed to speak with you about something," Molly said.

"Not at all. Here, let me take your coat." She unbuttoned her coat and handed it to him before slipping off her shoes and he then led her into the kitchen.

"Hello, Molly," Joan greeted her with an equally friendly smile, pouring out a cup of tea for Norman. "Would you like some tea?"

"Thank you." Molly sat down at the table and Norman resumed his place opposite.

"I want to speak to you about Aberdoch Manor," Molly began. "I'm afraid we have discovered it has severe wood rot, practically throughout the property."

"Goodness." Joan handed Molly a cup of tea.

"The problem is, we had two quotes that have been through the roof, excuse the pun," she paused with a ghost of a smile and then continued. "Auntie can't afford to pay to get it repaired. Well, she has half of the money but that's not good enough."

"Isn't your fiancé, Adam fixing the problem?" Norman enquired, stirring a second teaspoon of sugar into his tea.

"How did you know about Adam?" she asked, surprised.

"We bumped into Ross yesterday as he passed on his way to your place. I asked how it was going at Aberdoch after the flood and he told me about the wood rot. He said Adam was treating it. By the way, both Joan and I were thrilled to hear your fiancé is back, alive and well. What a wonderful surprise!"

Joan sat down at the table. "Yes, we couldn't believe it when Ross told us. Sad for Ross though, as I think he's rather fond of you," Joan said with a twinkle in her eye. "But you must be so delighted, Molly, to have Adam home at last with you."

"It's… it's not easy," Molly admitted. "Although of course, I'm glad he's alive and safe."

"Oh I can imagine it's not easy. War has had a terrible detrimental effect on many young men," said Joan, pouring herself a cup of tea from the teapot in the centre of the table.

"Yes," Molly replied, wondering just how much to tell them both. Was it morally right to tell the vicar and his wife she wanted to break off her engagement? "It's too much of a big job for Adam and it will put the opening time back for the hotel," she said, sticking to the subject of the wood rot. "To be honest, if we don't raise the money to pay a company to do it, I'm afraid Auntie will lose Aberdoch and everything she has invested in it so far."

"Gosh," Norman grimaced. "How much do you need?"

Molly pulled out the piece of paper she had ripped out from the notepad and showed him. "Goodness me!" Norman gasped, handing it to Joan to see. "I'm sorry Molly, but Joan and I don't have that kind of money."

"It wouldn't be all of it. Like I said, Auntie has half of the money."

Joan looked up from the piece of paper. "Does your aunt know you are here?" she asked cautiously. She felt quite sure Mrs Winters didn't. She would be far too proud to ask for help, especially from them.

"No," Molly replied reluctantly. "I just wanted to speak to you first about it."

"Clodagh, I'm not asking you to lie for me and I promise I'll be back long before supper." Ella stood near the front door pulling on her gloves.

Clodagh looked displeased. "Fergus was so very worried and for good reason too. You need to be slowing down with the bairn on the way."

"And I will, but I just need to help them through this outbreak of smallpox." She glanced in the mirror to check her hat. "I shan't be late," she said, walking out of the door.

Clodagh let out a sigh of hopelessness, there was no point trying to stop her, Ella was headstrong, she just hoped her generosity for helping others would not backfire on her. She rubbed the pain across her forehead as she walked back into the drawing room. She felt tired and generally off-colour - to be expected, she presumed, with the baby due soon.

Ella continued with her mission to help out at the hospital, despite Fergus' wishes for her never to return. Try as she might, she found it impossible to stay home, knowing she could be of help to those who needed her most. The hospital was in a state of chaos and smallpox was rapidly spreading throughout Dublin. It was on the third day of helping out and having successfully kept her secret safe with Clodagh, she had not accounted for the fact that Fergus could come home early as her carriage pulled up outside of Oaklands. The late afternoon sun was casting a golden glow over the lush grounds as a blackbird sang at the top of its voice and the sweet smell of soil after a recent shower filled the air. Ella stood for a moment, waiting for the clatter of the carriage to fade so that she could inhale the scented air and listen to the birdsong more clearly. It felt wonderfully peaceful after the mayhem she had faced since early that morning.

After a couple of minutes, and feeling calmer, she made her way up the steps and indoors.

Ross stared wildly vacant. Like a moth to a flame, he had gone back to the Ghost Tree again on a quest to know more about his past life with Ella. Perhaps seeing Ella would make him feel closer to Molly again. His heart ached for her.

"Where have you been?" Fergus dashed into the hallway to find Ella, having spotted her from one of the upstairs windows.

"I... uh..." she was taken aback. "Why are you home so soon, is everything alright at the mill?" she asked, in an attempt to throw him off track.

"Never mind that, it's Clodagh. It's just as well I did come back early, she's unwell, very unwell." He led the way upstairs to the bedroom. The room was in darkness and Ella pulled back the curtain slightly, letting in a little sunshine.

Molly left the vicarage feeling dejected. She had hoped

that Norman and Joan would be able to help, but unfortunately, they couldn't. Unless she could come up with another plan, there would be no other option than to let Adam do the work and keep the façade of her engagement going.

There was a wind picking up and the sky had become very grey and dull during the time she had been at the vicarage. She pulled up the collar of her coat and held it tightly as she made her way back through the fields. As she drew closer to the Ghost Tree, she could see a figure resting underneath its big old branches. She ran towards the tree and soon realised it to be Ross.

"Ross!" she patted his face, but there was no life, he was far away. "Oh Ross!" She knew his reason for going back was not only to find out more about their past lives, but for them to be together again. She missed him too - Fergus, Ross. They were one person living two different lives in two very different worlds. But no matter how different, the pain in her heart, the yearning to be with the man she truly loved, continued. She sat down next to him and kissed his cold cheek, wondering how long he was going to be lost in a trance. Then, with a strong overwhelming desire to join him, wherever he might be at that moment, she turned around and touched the inscribed heart, her hand fell into place on the rough, rugged trunk.

"Have you checked on the children?" Ella asked Fergus, turning away from Clodagh. Clodagh was red from fever and her lips were breaking out in sores.

"Yes, Lilly said she had a headache, Mary is fine and Ian is still at the mill with Michael."

Ella ran out of the room, down the hallway and into the children's room. Nanny, a young woman with mousey features and a pale complexion, stood up in surprise at Ella's sudden entrance with Fergus closely behind.

"Miss Lilly is complaining of a headache and she's feeling hot," Nanny said, apprehensively, watching Ella closely as she felt Lilly's forehead with the back of her hand.

"She has a fever too and I can see sores forming around her lips, just like Clodagh." Ella observed. "And Mary?" She walked over to the bed closest to the window. Mary was sleeping peacefully, but looking rather flushed with a rash on her arms.

"She was very tired today and seems a little hot," Nanny confirmed.

"Is it what I think it is?" Fergus faced Ella with anxiety rising from the pit of his stomach.

"I'm afraid so, it's smallpox. I'm guessing little Mary hasn't had it before, so she has caught it too by looks of that rash. What about you, Fergus have you had it?"

He shook his head. "I've never had it."

Then you must leave at once. She pushed him towards the bedroom door and then turned to face Nanny. "And you, Nanny, have you had it?"

"No," she replied with wide fearful eyes.

"Then you must wash and leave this house and don't come back for ten days. Do you understand?"

Not needing to be told twice, Nanny left the room in haste.

Ella found Fergus downstairs, pacing up and down nervously. "Fergus, you can't stay here in this house and neither can Michael or Ian, unless they've had this disease."

"I havenae a clue if either of them have, although I dinnae recall Ian having it. There's been workers at the mill going down with it, too."

"Michael must close the mill and you three should go and stay somewhere safe."

"I dinnae think he can close the mill, too many people's livelihoods depend on it."

"Well, whatever he decides, you must stay away from here. I'll take care of Clodagh and the girls. You know they will be in good hands with me."

"I ken that, but I worry about you too with overdoing it with the bairn on the way. Perhaps we should take them tae the hospital."

"They will not be able to do any more for them than I can, and they are overstretched as it is. If I am to save their lives, they will need around the clock care and here, I can give it to them. But I'll be sure to rest whenever I can," she added, pandering to his fretting.

"Uncle Fergus!" Ian's shouting sounded from outside in the courtyard. Fergus pulled back the curtain to see Michael hunched over, sitting on the bottom step vomiting violently.

"It's Michael" he said, fleeing out of the room to his cousin's aid.

"Fergus! Stop! Don't touch him and tell Ian not to. I'll help him." Ella rushed after Fergus.

Ross blinked hard and then coughed. He could feel his heart beating fast beneath his ribcage. It took a few seconds for him to realise he was no longer on the grounds at Oaklands but back in Aberdoch in 1946. He turned his head and saw Molly sitting next to him.

"Molly, what are you doing here?" She seemed to be staring right through him. "Molly!" He patted both sides of her face, but there was no getting through to her. The wind had gained strength as her hair whipped her flushed, cold cheeks. He stood up and looked down at her with despair, wondering what to do next. It felt like déjà vu, he had rescued her before when she had gone into a regression. He then remembered she had also ended up in hospital on one occasion, suffering from hypothermia. He felt her hands. They were ice cold, so he stuffed them both inside her pockets. He took off his scarf and placed it around her neck, high enough to cover her chin. He stood up again and ran anxious fingers through his hair. Should he go to Vicar Norman and Joan for help, as he had done previously? He hated to worry them. They had not understood last time and had thought Molly to be mentally ill or suffering from grief due to the loss of her fiancé. It was impossible to tell them what was really happening.

Despite Ella's protesting, Fergus helped Michael up to bed. Ian waited outside of the house as instructed by his aunt, although he was deeply worried about his little sister. But he knew there was nothing he could do, and if anyone could heal her, it would be Auntie Ella.

With everyone settled in their own rooms and Fergus having scrubbed his hands and arms well, he kissed Ella goodbye and left her to nurse the sick members of the

McDaniel family. Alfred had been instructed to leave plenty of firewood daily at the back door. Mrs O'Connor, the cook, having already had smallpox was to continue with her duties, although broth was probably only required for the sick if they could stomach it, but she knew she must look after Ella well and she would make other hearty meals for her.

Fergus had agreed reluctantly to stay away for at least a week until which time the illness would no longer be contagious. Ella closed the door behind him, hoping to God he and Ian would stay safe. It was going to be a challenging time ahead, probably the biggest she had faced alone so far in her medical capacity as a healer. There was no Jenny or Clara this time to help, as there had been during the Jacobite battles, no Amelia from the hospital and trained surgeons, it was just her and her alone to save those most precious to her. It carried a huge responsibility and one she only hoped she could fulfil.

Molly felt a little light headed as she rose to her feet. It was only as she began to walk away from the tree, did she see Ross in the distance. "Ross!" Her voice was lost in a gust of wind, and so she tried again. "Ross!" This time he heard her and turned around before sprinting back to her.

"Oh thank God. I was just off tae the vicarage to get help. You were completely out of it - I couldnae wake you."

"And so were you when I found you."

A soft smile crept over his lips. "What a pair we are."

He took her hands into his own. "Let me walk you back."

She nodded. "So, what did you see?" she asked, happy to be with him again. The warmth of his hand sent tingles of excitement through her body.

"It was not good," he said ruefully.

"Smallpox?"

"Aye, smallpox in the McDaniel household."

She stopped and faced him, knowing he had witnessed the same scenes as she had. "I don't think it's right, what we are doing." Her green eyes surveyed him closely.

"What's not right?"

"Seeing our past lives. They were hard times, Ross, upsetting and quite disturbing."

"Aye, of course they were, but don't you think that if we can learn from our mistakes back then, it could help us have a better life now?"

"Maybe, I don't know. Right now, knowing about our past is not going to help our current situation," she answered glumly. "I went to Vicar Norman to see if he might be able to help, you know, give Auntie a loan to fix the wood rot."

"Why?" Ross was confused. "I thought Adam was doing it. That's the whole reason why we are keeping *us* quiet."

"Yes, I know, but it's not easy, waiting for him to do it. It's a huge job. He's really changed, Ross. I feel like I don't know him, anymore. I never know what he's going to do or say next. He seems so angry and bitter most of the time. I know it's not his fault - he's ill - but I don't think he will ever be well again or ever be the same person he used to be."

"Would you want to him to be?"

"That's an unfair question."

"Is it?" Ross picked up her other hand and held them both tightly. "Molly, what we have is special, we are meant to be together, regardless, whether Adam gets well again or not."

"I know that. Of course I do. I didn't plan any of this… him coming back… me falling in love with you… knowing about Ella and Fergus, out past lives… it's hard, Ross."

"You fell in love with me more than two hundred years ago," he gave a wry smile. "If anyone deserves a chance it is us, me and you, I was your first love. Come on." He put his arm around her and they walked back together through the field.

"Where's Molly?" Adam asked Daphne, making his way back upstairs.

"Your guess is as good as mine. She said she was nipping out and has been gone ages. I've just had to sort out all the linen on my own." Daphne stood with her hands on hips looking up at him from the foot of the stairs.

"You should have said, I could have helped."

"I'd rather you help with the wood rot. How's it going?" She narrowed her eyes, waiting for his response. And after a moment's hesitation it came. "It's… it's coming along," he said, not sounding as convinced as she had hoped. "Are you sure about that?" Daphne replied, her thin, pencilled eyebrows knitting together.

He felt uneasy from her scrutinising gaze. "Yes, yes, of course. It's just that there's a lot to do so it will take me quite a while."

"Well, it will if you keep talking to me!" She shook her head and walked off.

"Of course. I'm getting back to it right now!" he called out, saluting her while her back was turned. He walked into one of the front facing bedrooms he had been working on and glanced out of the small squat window.

In the distance, he could see two figures walking through the fields. He screwed up his eyes, but being short-sighted these days, he didn't recognise them, probably a couple of locals out for a stroll. Admiring the land and countryside all around, he could imagine himself lord of the manor one day, when that miserable old bat died and Molly would inherit the place. As her husband, Aberdoch Manor would also be his. He grinned widely at the idea, but his reverie was short lived. The couple had stopped and were kissing passionately, and he suddenly had an uneasy feeling in his gut that something was not right. A moment later, they carried on walking, but this time they were no longer touching and as they left the field, he recognised them. Ross turned right and made his way to the garden and Molly continued towards the house. He could feel the colour rising in his cheeks and his nostrils flare in anger as he pounded his fist heavily down on the windowsill. So that was why she was keeping him at arm's length. She was carrying on with the gardener.

Chapter Nine

The trees in the grounds of Oaklands were full of blossom. Bunches of daffodils and crocuses had sprung up almost overnight, dotted around lush green lawns. Bees were hard at work, drifting from one flower to another, and butterflies and other insects were embracing mother nature's gift of spring after a long winter. The birds were in their element, breaking out into song, each in competition with the other. Yet despite this glorious scene of nature at its best, inside Oaklands, nature had been at its cruellest.

Ella stepped outside through the back door leading to the garden. Stricken with both grief and exhaustion, she flopped down on the step. And burying her face into her hands, she let out a heartfelt sob which in turn led to uncontrollable crying. She had kept it bottled up for too long and now the floodgates were open as her pain flowed out like a cascading waterfall of anguish and sorrow. She felt as if her heart was breaking in two, the ache was so deep she could feel it in the depths of her bones and her very soul. Too busy crying, she was oblivious to her surroundings, to the birdsong, the buzzing of the bees around the lavender bush she sat next to and even the clatter of the carriage as Fergus and Ian returned.

As the empty carriage headed off, Fergus stopped Ian from going inside of the house. He possessed a sixth sense something was dreadfully amiss. And then he heard her. He heard Ella's harrowing cries from the garden. "Ian, I need ye tae stay right here. Dinnae follow me, lad, until I come for you, do ye understand?"

Ian stared at him with fearful eyes. "But Uncle…"

"Lad, listen tae me, stay here." Fergus was firm and Ian knew it was wise not to argue.

"Ella." He stood before her and she looked up at him, forlorn and ashen.

"Oh Fergus." She stood up and he took her into his arms, letting her sob further for a while. Eventually, she looked up at him and it was clear to Fergus her crying was born out of grief. But he hardly dared to ask, whoever they had lost it would be tremendous. "Michael?" he asked solemnly, not being able to bear her reply if it was him. He couldn't imagine losing Michael, they had become so close lately.

She shook her head. "No, he's recovering well, so is little Mary."

For a second he felt a huge tidal wave of relief but it soon gave way to panic. "And Clodagh and Lilly?" He waited with bated breath for her reply. She couldn't find her words, instead she shook her head slowly, tears cascading once more.

He flung his hand to his mouth and for a moment, he thought he was going to be sick. "Oh, God, no… both of them?"

Her voice gave way to a small croak. "Yes."

His frantic eyes filled with tears. "No… no, this cannae be true." He stepped back from her, consumed with heartbreak. "I promised Shona. When I laid her tae rest I said I'd protect her bairns. And Clodagh, she was young, beautiful and with child. Michael… he must be…" He swallowed hard and wiped his tears. "How can I tell Ian he's lost his sister now too?"

Ella reached for his hands. "We will do it together."

He pulled his hands abruptly away from hers and

stood back with glazed eyes that were turning to anger. "You promised me… ye said you'd save them… you are the one that brought this illness tae our door, working in that hospital." He hissed the word hospital with spite.

"No! No I didn't. Fergus, listen to me, smallpox is all over Dublin… you said yourself workers at the mill had gone down with it too."

"I cannae… I cannae look at you just now." He walked away from her, leaving her sobbing and calling for him to come back.

Ross opened his eyes slowly, steadying his breathing, inhaling and exhaling deeply. He touched his face, realising it was wet from tears. He could still feel the deep ache in his heart, not only at the loss of Lilly and Clodagh, but the betrayal and hurt he believed Ella had brought upon him.

He rose to his feet, feeling a little shaky. Perhaps Molly was right, it was best he didn't know. He feared when he next saw Molly, he would still feel the resentment he carried towards Ella. He chided himself inwardly, remembering that Molly was no longer Ella and he was no longer Fergus. There was a reason why we were not supposed to remember our past lives, and he was now finding out it was better to leave the past where it belonged. Although the question remained, if he could resist the urge to go back one last time. A part of him wanted to know if Fergus and Ella would have their happy ending and if they would get past what he had just seen. Could Fergus forgive her? And was it really Ella's fault? Surely, she had done her best to save Lilly and Clodagh.

"There you are!" Molly found Adam in the back yard, sawing wood for the new rafters in the roof to replace the ones where the wood rot had caused so much damage that it was impossible to salvage.

Adam looked up and wiped his brow with the back of his hand. Every time he looked at her, he could see her kissing Ross, and it pained him, but so far, he had kept quiet and surprisingly, managed to keep his cool. He needed to play the long game and win her back without her even realising, yet charm or patience was not something he possessed much of.

"Auntie says we can have dinner in half an hour, if you'll be able to finish off now and get cleaned up?"

"Yes, that's fine, getting arm ache anyway," he said, placing the saw down, then bending his right arm back and forth, demonstrating his point.

"You're out of practice," Molly smiled.

"Out of practice?" He looked at her blankly.

"Yes… being a carpenter, you were doing this kind of stuff every day before the war, weren't you?"

"Ah right… yes… get your meaning now." He flashed a reassuring smile. "Molly, I was wondering, as I've not seen anywhere other than this beautiful house of course, but maybe you could show me around, take me to that tearoom you spoke of the other night? Or that village hall that serves as a pub? I could do with a pint of beer."

"Uh… yeah… of course. Although Auntie wants you to crack on with the roof first, so it won't be any time soon, I'm afraid."

"Surely, she doesn't expect me to work seven days a week? It's nearly weekend, I'm sure she'd give me Sunday off, at least."

"This is Aunt Daphne we are talking about, she doesn't believe in Sunday being a day of rest. She's on a mission to get this wood rot sorted as soon as possible so that we can open the hotel." If truth be told, Molly knew full well if she or Adam were to ask her for Sunday off or Saturday evening to go for a drink, she would have agreed, wishing to keep Adam sweet, if nothing else, but Molly would rather paint the picture of her being a tyrant; it played more in her favour. What if she were to bump into Ross? It would be incredibly awkward. Also, she didn't want to have to introduce Adam to the locals; he wasn't going to be staying around long enough with any luck, and least of all would she want them to know he was her fiancé.

"Right." He knew she was brushing him off; he wasn't stupid.

Molly did feel a little guilty, looking at the dejection in his eyes, but she didn't wish to lead him on. "Maybe some time when the job is done," she said, half-heartedly. "Adam, you never did say what happened between you and your parents. Why did they chuck you out?"

He seemed taken aback by her question and sudden change of topic. "Oh... I..." He began stacking the wood behind him to avoid eye contact with her. "They didn't exactly chuck me out," he admitted. "I left of my own accord."

"But I thought..."

"I walked out because I found it too hard work," he cut in. "They kept speaking about the past, about Graham, it was painful not being able to remember, not even remember my own brother."

Molly gave a small sigh of relief, at least he did have somewhere to go, a family who loved him when the time came for him to leave Aberdoch Manor. "I understand, but I'm sure they must be very worried about you. Have you had any contact with them since you've been here? You can always use the telephone. Why don't you call them after dinner? At least let them know you're safe."

"No!" Adam retorted. "Just… just leave it, Mol. This is none of your business."

"Right, yes of course, your family is none of my business." She stepped back from him and turned to walk away.

"Molly, wait!"

She span around in anticipation, waiting for an apology.

"Stop pushing me, alright? I'm a grown man and I'll decide if I want them in my life or not, and right now, I don't."

"Fine!" she replied curtly, before walking off back to the house.

Ian hugged and rocked his little cousin to sleep, consumed in his own grief too. First, he lost his father when he was very young - the scenes of his father being executed by the Red Coats were still vivid in his mind - then recently his mother and those images of her falling to her death down the stairs were raw and painful, and now his sister, Lilly, had lost her life to smallpox. It felt like all those he loved had left him, apart from his aunt and uncle and his new found cousins. He felt sorry for Cousin Michael losing Clodagh and their unborn child, and now poor Mary only had her father. He lay her down gently on the bed, and pulled the covers over her, and then walked out of the room and into his own. Lilly's bed was neatly made up and her dolly sat propped up on the pillow. He walked over to it and picked it up, bringing it close to his face. He could still smell her, still see in his mind's eye her carrying it around everywhere she went, ever since leaving Aberdoch. It had been a comfort to her, a reminder of her mother and the home she had left behind. He let out a heartfelt sob and dropped down onto her bed, crying. The ache of losing her was coupled by the same ache he possessed for the loss of his parents and he wondered if he would ever come to terms with losing them all. It was a cruel world and a part of him wished he could have died with them; at least they would all be together.

A tangible silence filled the air as Ella, Fergus and Michael attempted to dine. Michael struggled to eat anything, it was the first meal he had tried to eat in over a week, and the first time he had felt it possible to come downstairs and sit at the dining table.

"Don't worry if you can't manage much, a little is better than nothing," Ella smiled softly, looking at his pale face and his eyes encompassed with dark circles.

He nodded, grateful for her caring words. He held no grudge, unlike Fergus. He knew Ella had done everything in her power to help Clodagh and Lilly.

"I don't want ye tae worry about anything, Cousin." Fergus reached out and touched his shoulder with affection. "I've told them at the mill and they all send their deepest condolences. I've also confirmed the funeral is on Wednesday…" He swallowed the lump at the back of his throat, trying to contain his emotions.

"They'll both be laid to rest together?" Ella asked, making sure she had understood correctly.

He stared back at her with eyes of steel. "Aye, they will be."

"Will it be in the morning?"

"Aye, it will. Why, do ye have somewhere else you'd rather be? Do ye wish tae visit the hospital, is that it?" he glared at her with so much anger.

She shrunk back in her chair. "No, I gave you my word I wouldn't return.

"It's a bit late for that now. Ye should have kept yer word before... ye could have spared three lives, if ye had."

"That's enough, Fergus!" Michael threw down his knife and fork. "Ella is no at fault. There's no proof she brought that illness into our home. I... you and I... and even Ian... mixed with workers at the mill and could have brought it back."

"But maself and Ian didnae have it, did we?"

"No, but I did and more than half the workforce have gone down with it, many will have lost their lives. What's done is done, and being angry is no helping the matter. No amount of anger is going tae bring back ma wife... or ma... " He wiped his tears, "ma unborn child."

Ella reached out and touched Michael's hand. "We will do everything we can to help you and Mary, I promise."

"You're grieving too, both of yous," he said, glancing first at Fergus and then back at Ella. "You need each other, dinnae shut one another out. Dinnae throw away the love ye have because God knows, I wish I still had ma wife, ma beautiful Clodagh by ma side. You still have each other."

Fergus blinked against the sting of his tears and then reached out for Ella's hand. He was aware that he had been lashing out, feeling the need to blame someone for this awful fate that had been cast upon them yet again. He blamed the McKenzies for the loss of his sister and the clan, they were responsible for those deaths but Ella wasn't responsible for Lilly and Clodagh's. Michael was right to spell it out to him. She got up, and walked around the table and hugged them both. The three of them held each other for a long time, trying to find some kind of comfort in each other's arms. It was going to be a long road ahead, picking up the pieces, and to do so they needed to draw strength from each other, united as a family.

Chapter Ten

Adam, standing on a ladder on the landing, glided a gentle hand over a wooden beam. The moment he touched it, it began to crumble away. He cursed under his breath; the treatment he had bought didn't seem to be working. He moved his hand further up the beam and a large chunk of rotten wood fell into his palm, just as Molly walked passed. She looked up at him with concern. "That's not good."

"Expert on wood rot, are you, Molly?"

"No, but you don't need to be an expert to see how bad that is."

"Very observant. Of course, it's bad."

"Why do you have to be like that?"

He climbed down the ladder and faced her. "Like what?"

"So... uppity."

"Uppity? Is that even a proper word?" he scoffed.

"Yes, it is, for your information. Look it up in the dictionary." She walked off leaving him watching her as she made her way downstairs. He sighed heavily. He was getting tired; she was hard work. He glanced back up at the wooden beams - and so was the wood rot.

The phone rang just as Molly reached the bottom stair. She walked over to the highly polished oak desk and the ringing black phone, then picked up the receiver. "Aberdoch Manor." She put on her best telephone voice and smiled inwardly, thinking how much she sounded like her mother whenever she answered the phone.

"Aberdoch Manor, Molly Hazleton speaking, how may I help you?" She needed to practise for when the hotel was up and running.

"Ah, Molly, just the person I need to speak to, it's Norman here." His friendly voice echoed down the line.

"Vicar Norman, hello."

Upstairs, the clatter of the ladder forced Molly to look up. She caught sight of Adam mimicking her, *"Vicar Norman, hello."* He walked off with the ladder under his arm into another room. She rolled her eyes and brought her attention back to Norman on the other end of the line.

"I was wondering if you had time to pop round later today, perhaps at four o'clock? I have an idea that might help you, regarding your predicament."

"Predicament?" she echoed, wondering what he meant, and then it dawned on her that he was probably referring to her need of a loan. "Oh, the money, you mean?" she said in a hushed tone, so as no one would hear.

"Yes, I might have a solution about that," Norman replied. Joan hovered next to Norman, mouthing the word *cake* to him. "Joan has made a fruit cake, she said to tell you."

"Lovely," Molly smiled down the phone, happier about the possibility of being able to raise the money for the wood rot than Joan's cake of course, but if cake was on offer too, even better! "I'll be there at four."

"We look forward to it." Norman put the receiver down, feeling pleased.

Joan placed the fruit cake on a plate and cut it into equal slices. The kettle let off a loud whistle just as the door knocked. Norman, making his way from the living room, nearly tripped over Carrot as the cat jumped off his lap and ran full speed in front of him, then, as he pulled opened the door, he darted outside. "Come in Molly, ignore Carrot, he's having one of his loopy moments." He ushered her inside and took her coat. She smiled gratefully and slipped off her shoes. "Go through," he said, pointing in the direction of the living room.

Molly sat down on the sofa and a moment later Joan appeared with a silver tray containing tea and cake as promised. "Lovely to see you, Molly. How have you been?" Joan served her a cup of tea.

"Fine, thank you. Busy," she replied. What she really wanted to say was awful, missing Ross, and Adam was driving her mad, not to mention the worry of them fixing the wood rot and the prospect of the hotel ever opening seemed less likely by the day. Instead, she put on a brave face and hoped they might be able to help after all.

Norman resumed his place in his favourite armchair and Joan sat down in the one next to him.

"So, about your money problem," Norman began. "We are currently raising funds for the church roof, there's a small leak that is getting worse every time it rains."

"Which is practically every day. It never rains but it pours!" Joan chortled.

"Indeed," Norman smiled.

Molly was hanging on his every word.

"We are extremely lucky because the parishioners have been so very generous. We've been collecting for quite some time, so you see we have some money over in the pot. When that happens, we use it for other things, such as new books for example, or church events or even donate it to charity. We only replaced the books six months ago and I can't think of anything better to spend it on than…"

"You would like to give it to us… for Aberdoch Manor?" Molly asked with wide eyes.

Joan nodded her head and Norman said, "yes, but I'm afraid it's not enough, so we thought about having a church fair."

"Vicar Norman," Molly interrupted, "as grateful as I am, Auntie would be mortified to think we would be considered as some kind of charity. She's a proud woman, and so am I, come to think of it."

"Oh, no," Joan intercepted. "Norman wasn't implying that at all, were you Dear?"

"No, certainly not," Norman agreed. "What I was about to say was that the church supports charities but also local businesses that require help. For instance, the post office was in desperate need of a renovation…"

"It was practically crumbling around their ears," Joan added.

"But Jaqueline and Gary McKenzie were struggling, as many people were during wartime. The locals didn't want to see the post office close down, it would have meant us having to go all the way to Eyemouth, so we held an event and raised money for them. The church donated a big chunk of it and we saved the post office from closing."

"That's wonderful," said Molly. "But I don't think the locals are keen on us opening a hotel in the first place, given the horrible history of the place, so I can't imagine them wanting to help."

"You'd be surprised. If it boosts the economy and brings business to the post office, the corner shop, the pub at the village hall, the tearoom, they'll be all for the idea. As for the history of Aberdoch Manor, it is not your fault and it's about time someone did something with the place. It needs a happy future."

"Do you really think so?" Molly asked, feeling more positive again.

Joan flashed a reassuring smile. "Oh yes, Norman is

right, aren't you Dear?"

"Absolutely, which is why I'm suggesting it."

"So do you think a fair will raise the rest of the money we need?"

Norman pushed his glasses back up his nose. "It will help and then if there's any shortfall, I should be able to give you a personal loan for the remainder."

"Really? Oh gosh, I don't know what to say." Molly sat forward, excitedly. She would kiss him if she thought it appropriate, but of course it wasn't the done thing to kiss the vicar. Instead she thanked him and Joan with a beaming smile and tears in her eyes. They had just answered her prayers.

"So, we were thinking it probably best to leave your aunt out of all this," Joan said tactfully. "That way we can find a way to give her the money without her feeling... well, you know..."

"Embarrassed. Yes, absolutely," Molly agreed. The last thing she wanted was Daphne saying no to be stubborn. "A church fair wouldn't really be Auntie's thing, anyway," said Molly.

"Um, I suspected that," Norman agreed, imagining Daphne causing havoc, being rude to all and sundry.

"Do you like baking, Molly?" Joan asked with anticipation.

"Yes, I used to bake with my mum a lot, we have a big kitchen in our farmhouse."

"Oh how wonderful! Well, I thought we could make some cakes, scones, pastries, that sort of thing, to sell. We could work together on it, if you like."

"Yes, definitely. I honestly can't thank you both enough." Her eyes brimmed with tears again, grateful that at last she could see a way out of the mess she was in. It really was the answer to her problems and Daphne's too.

After finishing a second slice of cake and a third cup

of tea, Molly left the vicarage wearing a big smile. The sun was shining brightly to match her happiness as she walked back through the fields. She stopped for a moment at the Ghost Tree. A robin sat on a lower branch; its chirpy song made Molly smile even more. For the first time in a long while, she felt like things were going to be alright. It was as if the dark cloud that had been looming over her ever since Christmas was finally lifting. Even the weather seemed milder than it had been in months. She stood for a moment looking at the carved heart on the tree, wondering about Fergus and Ella. Did they ever get their happy ending? She hoped they did and she hoped it continued into this life, and she would get her happy ending with Ross. She sighed wistfully and then walked on, quickening her pace, eager to go and find Ross and tell him the good news.

Ross was shifting rocks from one side of the garden to another with the aid of a wheelbarrow, ready to build a rockery in the morning. He was startled by the firm hand that grabbed his shoulder. He turned around to see Adam standing in front of him.

"I think it's time you and I had a little chat," he said, coolly.

Ross stood up and faced him. "Oh aye, what about?"

"I think you know what about… Molly."

Ross kept his expression neutral, not wanting to show the fact he felt intimidated by Adam's hard stare.

"What's the deal between you both?"

"Deal?" Ross looked at him blankly. He wanted to say the deal is I'm madly in love with her and you need to back off and leave Aberdoch right now. But he knew how important it was to Molly and Daphne that he stayed and finish his job at Aberdoch Manor.

"Are you in love with her?" he asked, catching Ross

off guard again.

"What makes ye think that?"

"Oh let's see, maybe the fact that your tongue was down her throat a few days ago!"

"What? Don't be daft. Look I've got work tae be getting on with and I would have thought you had too." Ross walked away from him, and Adam quickened his pace.

"This conversation isn't over. I want to know the truth. I need to know... are you in love with her?... yes or no?" There was an air of desperation in his tone.

"It's none of yer business," Ross replied harshly. "If she was truly happy with you, ye wouldnae need tae fret about me. I'd no be a threat tae ye."

"You're not a threat to me. I just want to know what your intentions are, because if I should leave, I don't want her being left to someone who isn't going to treat her right."

"Rich, coming from you," Ross scoffed. "I would never treat Molly the way you do. She deserves so much better than you," he said scornfully. "And aye, I do love her."

"Right." Adam looked away from him, hiding his emotions before walking off and leaving Ross wondering what the reason was behind the conversation they had just had. What did he mean by if he was to leave? Was he thinking of going? He also expected Adam to land him a punch, seeing as he had just confessed to loving Molly, but instead he turned the other cheek and left. Odd. Very odd.

Molly had spotted Adam heading back indoors just as she reached the edge of the field. She took the back route behind the house that led to the gardens, to avoid anyone seeing her. In front of her she could see Ross walking along with a ladened wheelbarrow. She gave a small whistle to gain his attention as she stood near an outbuilding. He stopped and turned around, spotting her immediately. She beckoned him over with a coy smile and he left his wheelbarrow and went over to her. She immediately pulled him forcefully into what used to be the old stables and kissed him passionately.

"Wow!" he said eventually. "I wasnae expecting that."

"I miss you," she said. "And I have some good news."

"Don't tell me… Adam's leaving?"

She frowned. "How do you know that?" She hadn't even told Adam yet that his services were no longer needed, not for the wood rot and not as her fiancé either.

"He gave the impression just now when he came tae ask me if I'm in love with you?"

"He did what? Why?"

"I think he might have seen us kissing."

"When?" Molly looked horrified. "I didn't want him to find out like that. I wanted to sit down with him and explain everything, let him down gently."

Ross was confused. "I thought that was why he was leaving, because you'd had words with him."

"No, not yet, but I will soon because I've just come from the vicarage and, well, Vicar Norman and Joan are helping me raise the money! We already have half of it for the wood rot and the other half we are going to raise with a church fair next week."

"Oh, I see. So Adam doesn't know yet?"

"No. I thought I'd wait until I have the money. If he goes now, Auntie will have a fit and will be worried sick about not affording to fix the wood rot."

"Well just tell her what you told me."

"I can't do that. If she knew the money was coming from Vicar Norman and he is behind the fundraising, she wouldn't accept the money, she's far too proud."

"Well she's going to have to know sooner or later," Ross pointed out.

"Yes, but I'm hoping I will come up with a way of avoiding that. Maybe pay the company before she has a chance to say no, either way, isn't it good news?"

"Absolutely!" He beamed, lifting her off her feet, as she shrieked and they kissed again.

The church bells were still ringing, slowly and solemnly, as Ella, Fergus, Michael, Ian and little Mary left the graveyard, dressed in black. The sky was dark and threatening rain, matching their sombre moods as they got into a waiting carriage and made their way back to Oaklands. Clodagh with her unborn child and Lilly were now laid to rest in the grounds of St Audoen's Church; the same church where Michael and Clodagh married and Mary was christened.

Somehow, the remaining McDaniels had to find a way to move on with their lives but it felt like an impossible task, one that none of them could find the strength to contemplate on such a tragically sad day. All they wanted to do was go home and grieve.

Slowly, the days turned into weeks and Michael found comfort in being back at the mill with Fergus, and so did Ian. Ian preferred to keep busy and the men had him running over town collecting rags for the mill, which left Ella looking after Mary with the help of Nanny, who was back at work now after recovering from smallpox. There was no chatter or laughter that once filled the house; it was as if the ones left behind just existed from day to day, doing what they had to do to survive. Mary was quiet and withdrawn and missed her mother dreadfully; her only little bit of happiness was when Ian came back from the mill. They had grown close, forming more of a sibling relationship than distant cousins. He was the brother she never had and she was the sister he had lost, and as the only children at Oaklands, despite their age difference, they understood each other and found comfort from one another.

Ella spent many hours staring out of the window, thinking about the hospital and how she missed putting her healing skills to good use, but her thoughts always drifted back to the fact that she had failed to heal Lilly and Clodagh. She felt like she was carrying a huge burden, consumed with guilt, despite Fergus now realising she was not at fault and neither he nor Michael blamed her, but nevertheless she blamed herself. It seemed that trouble followed her wherever she went. As if it wasn't enough that the Red Coats were after her for crimes she hadn't committed, she now had to live with the guilt that she wasn't able to save Lilly and Clodagh and her unborn child. And in a month from now, her own first child would be born. She only hoped it would bring comfort and joy back into the house and draw them all closer as a family once more.

Chapter Eleven

"What time will you be back?" Daphne frowned.

"Auntie, I am entitled to a day off sometimes, aren't I?" Molly slipped on her coat and shoes.

"Yes, of course you are, but why you want to spend it at the vicarage, baking with old Mrs Fusspot, is beyond me."

"I told you, she's baking for the church fair and could do with a hand."

"And she doesn't have anyone else to help her?" Daphne pursed her lips. "I find that hard to believe. I'm sure one of the church cronies would be eager enough."

"Well, yes, she probably can find someone else to help, but it's just that I told her I miss baking with my mum," Molly lied, trying to throw her off scent; the less she knew the better and it was only a little white lie afterall.

"Well if that's the case, I could arrange for you to bake with Mrs Brady. I'd offer myself but I can't stand up for hours in the kitchen with my hip these days."

"No, it's fine, Auntie. I don't know why you dislike me spending time at the vicarage."

"They're strange people… besides, you need friends your own age."

"They're not strange, they're good people and you will see that soon enough." Molly left the room, leaving Daphne with a frown on her face.

"See that soon enough… see what?" she called out, but Molly was already gone.

By midday, Joan and Molly had completed all the baking and promptly packed boxes of cupcakes, Victoria sandwich cakes, biscuits and scones and loaded them onto the back seat of the car. Norman had walked to church that morning to help set up the stalls so that Joan could use the car.

"I think we've done an amazing job." Joan smiled broadly, glancing back at the boxes on the back seat.

"I think so, too," Molly agreed. "It was fun."

Joan started the engine. "Well, let's hope the fruits of our labour pay off."

"I'm sure they will. Who is going to be able to resist them?" Molly grinned. It felt good to be doing something away from Aberdoch Manor for a change and especially as it was for a great cause… to save Aberdoch Manor. At least they will no longer have to rely on Adam. She planned on speaking to him tomorrow morning, just as soon as she knew for sure she had the money, or as close as.

Eyemouth 1746

A mist had rolled in, covering Eyemouth Harbour as fishing boats drifted in with their day's catch. A row of ponies stood tethered outside of The Wee Bonnie Duck Tavern. Inside, it was busy for a Tuesday afternoon. Agnes ran from one side of the bar to the other, filling tankards with ale and handing out wine and whisky. Clan McKenzie were sitting in the far corner of the dimly lit room, plotting and scheming their next Jacobite move. Jack McKenzie got up and walked towards a poster that had caught his eye. He pulled it off the wall, laughing loudly. "Hamish, I see yer wee sassenach wench is still on the run!" He held up a pencil sketch of Ella with the words *wanted for witchcraft and two counts of murder written* above her head.

"Aye, thanks tae this pathetic lot." He glared at their pale faces sitting around the table. The Aberdoch Manor massacre was still a sore subject. Hamish had expressed his anger freely by punishing them with a brutal whipping one by one the very next day. "Had ye done yer job properly," he hissed, "she and Fergus McDaniel wouldnae have got away. He'd be dead and she'd be mine, tae pleasure me on these cold winter nights." A hint of an evil grin appeared on his lips, thinking of her. They shrank back into their chairs, doing their best not to look him in the eyes.

A scruffy, overweight man with a matted, coppery beard, sitting at the next table, stood up. "How much is it worth tae ye, tae ken where they are?" He raised a bushy brow.

"Ye ken where they are?" Hamish's tone was one of surprise as he stood up and walked towards him.

"Aye, I might," the man replied candidly, now regretting opening his mouth, as Hamish's big frame towered above him. His hands were huge and he suspected they were capable of murder.

"Well either ye do or ye dinnae ken where they are," he said bluntly.

"I wouldnae mess wi' him," Jack advised. "He's no bonnie when he's angry." Jack frowned and said mockingly, "although, come tae think of it, he's no bonnie when he isnae either."

"Aye, I do ken where they are," he replied, acting on Jack's advice while plucking up more courage. "For a price, I'll tell ye."

Hamish let out a short raucous laugh. He took out a black pouch from his sporran and pulled out a silver coin, then handed it to the man.

"Make it two and we have a deal," he said, trying his luck.

"Ye'll take the one or I'll snap yer neck and that'll be the end."

"And if ye do that, ye'll never find out where they are," he replied, standing his ground.

The others had now gathered around Hamish, waiting for his response, well aware that no one gets away with messing with Hamish McKenzie. But to everyone's surprise, he pulled out another coin and handed it to him. He looked over his shoulder at his clan with annoyance. "Sit down, this is for ma ears only. He turned and faced the man again. "Start speaking."

"I saw them getting on a boat destined for Dublin."

"Dublin, ye say?" Hamish screwed up his eyes, scrutinising the man. "And yer certain it was them?"

"Aye, she," he pointed to the poster, "was with a man, tall with red hair, and two children of the same colouring. It was definitely Dublin they were heading."

"So they have an Irish connection," Hamish mumbled through his beard.

Without warning, he grabbed the man by the throat and pinned him up against the wall. "If ye're no telling me the truth, I'll be back for ma money and then I'll chop off some precious parts of yer body before I finally kill ye."

The room fell silent as all eyes were on Hamish. Not wanting to bring too much attention to the subject of Ella's disappearance, he placed the man back down on his feet. "And dinnae breathe a word tae naebody," he whispered in his ear, "including the Red Coats, do ye hear me?"

"Aye," the man nodded vigorously, clearly shaken up. "I'll no tell a soul, ye have ma word."

The sun came out at lunchtime, just as the fair got under way. It was buzzing with locals and people from the highlands and even as far as Eyemouth. Word had spread far and wide, thanks to Joan and some of the regulars at church handing out leaflets everywhere they went. There were lots of stalls, ranging from arts and crafts, handmade jewellery, paintings, food and local produce. There were raffles, tombola and various games and activities for the children.

Norman patted Molly proudly on the shoulder. "Couldn't have expected a better turnout. And Molly, these cupcakes look delicious." He dived a hand over the table, helping himself.

"Norman Fisher, where's your money?" Joan held out her palm expectantly, with half a smile.

Molly laughed at Joan. "Surely as the organiser he should get one for free?"

"Absolutely not," Joan was sticking to her guns.

"It's quite alright, Molly, I always pay my bills." He pulled out a couple of coins and dropped them into the payment jar, then promptly sank his teeth into the iced covered cupcake in his hand. Joan spotted someone she had not seen in a long time and dashed off, while Norman continued chomping his cake.

Ross walked towards Molly, impressed. "This is amazing, I've never seen an event so busy, well not since our own VE Day celebration. They really must want to save Aberdoch Manor."

"I can't think why, but I'm enormously grateful for their support," Molly replied, just as delighted at the turn out.

"Dinnae flatter yerself, they're no doing this for you," said Iris McKenzie, suddenly appearing from behind them both. "Folk round these parts welcome any social event, seeing as its dead boring most of the year. Even if it means raising money tae save the house of horrors... any excuse for a bit of fun." She threw a look of distaste at Molly.

"That's enough, Iris," Ross scolded.

"Well, I'm just saying. She thinks she's so prim and proper, she's just a sassenach who turns up here with her old aunt. And the old bag cannae even be bothered tae show her face while everyone else has to gather round and cough up tae save the frigging roof of that run-down oversized ghost house."

"Iris, I said that's enough!" Ross grabbed her arm, but Molly stepped in, having heard more than enough. "Ross, let go." He released his grip.

"Firstly, it is due to your ancestors massacring Clan McDaniel that you call it the house of horrors. Being a McKenzie is nothing to be proud of." She returned Iris' hostile glare.

"Poppycock! You need tae learn the history around here. The McKenzies were doing their duty, having been asked by the king to rid of the McDaniels because they were trouble. Shame they didnae do it properly or he wouldnae be here today." She flashed an angry look at Ross.

"You're a nasty piece of work. A true McKenzie through and through." Ross gritted his teeth, seething. If Iris had been a man, he would have given her what she deserved.

"I'll take that as a compliment." She tsked and flicked her long hair over her shoulders, turning around to walk off.

"And for the record, my aunt doesn't know about this fair because the money is meant to be a surprise, that's why she's not here."

"Who gives a toss, ye both should go back tae where yous come from." She strode off.

"Molly pulled Ross back. "Don't, she's not worth it." Suddenly Iris' attitude brought back a flashback to Molly from long ago. It had been late at night. Clan McDaniel were heading back to Aberdoch Manor after a long and weary journey. Travelling with them was Jack McKenzie, having been separated from his own men in Carlisle. Shona had put on a feast for them all and Fergus asked Jack to stay and give a chance for his weary horse to rest. Jack threw the kind gesture back at Fergus with insults. He had refused flatly to let the horse rest, spitting at his feet, before riding off into the darkness. His insolent behaviour reminded Molly of Iris. Iris was a female version of Jack, she even looked like him, Molly realised.

"You shouldn't have told her yer aunt doesnae know about the fair," said Ross, dragging her attention back to the present.

"Why? Will she tell her?" Molly looked at Ross with worried eyes.

"I wouldnae put it past her." Ross sighed.

Chapter Twelve

Molly was aware of the telephone ringing downstairs as she woke from a confusing dream. Fergus had been beckoning her to come back to him. She had been walking towards the Ghost Tree, following him. But no matter how quickly she ran, she couldn't seem to catch up with him. Behind her, Ross and Adam were calling her, pleading for her to come back to them. Their voices echoing in her ears were replaced by the high pitch of the telephone and then Daphne's shrill. "Molly! Molly are you up yet?"

Molly grabbed her dressing gown that had fallen on the floor next to the bed and flung it around herself, while stuffing her feet into her slippers. "Coming!" She made her way downstairs.

"It's your mother," Daphne said, cupping her hand over the receiver. "She didn't say what it was about, only that it's urgent. She's insisting on speaking to you first."

Molly frowned deeply. Daphne passed her the phone.

"Mum, is it Dad?" Molly's voice became panicked. "Is something wrong with Emily, Henry, Charlie?"

"No, we're all fine," Ruth said, calming her. "A telegram came for you. As you weren't here, I opened it on your behalf."

"I don't understand, telegram from who?" Molly said, baffled.

"It's about Adam."

"Adam? Are his parents searching for him? I did tell him to call them but he wouldn't listen."

"Darling, listen to me." Ruth's voice echoed with concern down the line. "Are you sitting down?"

"No, I'm standing. Why?" Molly asked, feeling confused. Her mother wasn't making any sense and if it wasn't so early in the morning, she'd have sworn she had been on the cooking sherry.

"Please sit down," Ruth insisted.

Molly went behind the desk and sat down. "Right, I'm sitting, can we get on with this now? Who's the telegram from?"

"The Home Office. Darling, they found Adam's body. A mass grave was discovered in France. It has taken them many weeks to identify the bodies but…"

"Well they've obviously made a mistake," Molly chuckled without humour. "Adam is here with me, you know he is, I told you when he arrived. And you saw him yourself at Christmas."

"Molly, he's not Adam."

Molly's head began to spin and for a moment she thought she might faint. Her heart skipped a beat. "What do you mean, he's not Adam?"

"What is it?" Daphne asked impatiently. "What's she said to upset you? Give me the phone." Daphne snatched the phone from Molly.

"Ruth, now listen here. I don't know what you've said to the poor girl but she's turned as white as a sheet. What's going on?"

Molly took three deep breaths in and out, steadying her nerves. This couldn't be happening, surely not. In a moment she would wake up and realise it was all a bad dream.

Daphne grabbed hold of the desk for more support, the pain in her hip was bringing her much discomfort this morning. "You mean to say we've got an imposter under our roof? My God, he could be anyone, a common criminal for all we know."

Molly ran off upstairs. She flew down the corridor and bust into Adam's room. It was empty. His bed was neatly made, curtains open. She ran over to the wardrobe and flung open the doors. Empty. She then spotted an envelope resting on the windowsill. She picked it up and ripped it open in haste and read it, before running full speed downstairs just as Daphne hung up the phone. "He left this." She shoved the note into Daphne's hand.

Dear Molly, I'm sorry but I can't do this anymore, I'm not the person you think I am. X Daphne huffed. "And he had the cheek to even put a kiss, but I see he didn't sign it."

"This can't be happening. How could I be so stupid? How could I not know my own fiancé?"

"You mustn't blame yourself, he's a con man, good at fooling people. I mean your parents, even Emily, Henry, Charlie, they all believed it was Adam too. They believed his surgery story, he must be a dead ringer for him."

"But I should have known," Molly cried. "And all that time Adam… Adam was lying in a ditch, dead. Oh my God Auntie, I feel sick! Poor Adam."

"Now, come on, let's go and get a nice cup of tea." She placed a comforting arm around Molly's shoulders and led her in the direction of the kitchen.

The train came to a grinding halt at the end of the platform. Henry waited at the only exit as the passengers disembarked and hurried on their way. At the far end he spotted him. He inhaled deeply then exhaled trying to keep his cool. As he came closer, Henry pulled down his cap and stood back so as not to be noticed, and as he passed him, he followed him until they were away from the crowds. He quickened his pace and then grabbed his arm, swinging him unexpectedly around to face him.

"You bastard!" Henry swung a hard punch straight on the nose and he fell back. It took a moment for him to recognise Henry and when he did, realising he was Molly's brother, he swallowed hard. "I deserved that... I know I did."

"You deserve more than that, but first I want an explanation. Who the bloody hell are you and why were you pretending to be my sister's fiancé?"

A woman pushing a pram passed by, nervously eyeing both the men with suspicion.

Henry grabbed his arm again. "Not here, let's go somewhere more private." He led him out of the street and down a small alleyway at the back entrance of the Red Lion pub.

"Right, start talking. What's your name?"

He wiped the blood away from his nose with the cuff of his jacket. "Matthew Hawley. I was in the same regiment as Adam. They called me Adam's twin. It was never Matthew's twin, always Adam's." His tone was bitter and full of resentment. "He had it all. A family who cared for him, a fiancée who wrote to him without fail... I read his letters when he wasn't around, they were so full of love."

"And let me guess... You have nothing, no family, no girl to call your own so you thought you'd steal his? Steal a dead man's fiancée?" Henry was struggling to find any pity for him.

"Pretty much, yeah. I never knew my parents. I was abandoned by my birth mother in a box outside the police station. I grew up in a home with boys pissing on me for fun, bullying me, smacking my head against the wall or flushing it down the bog. When I left school, I worked as an errand boy in a corner shop where the boss never stopped shouting and having a go at me. I then worked at a public house and was set upon by a gang of thugs who beat the shit out of me one night on my way home and that's where my scar on my chin came from." He lifted his chin and pointed to it. "It wasn't surgery during the war. When war broke out, I was the first to sign up, in the hope I'd be the first to get shot and killed."

Henry narrowed his eyes, watching him closely, trying not to fall in the trap of feeling sorry for him, but he had to admit it was quite a hard luck story.

"My whole life has been a bloody joke." Tears brimmed his stinging red eyes. "I couldn't even manage that…to get shot!"

"So when Adam did, you thought you'd help yourself to his life, is that it?" Henry regretted his harsh tone but couldn't help it. If it had happened to anyone else, he might have been more sympathetic but he had made a fool out of his sister, the whole family, in fact.

Matthew fell silent with his head hung low in shame.

"Well?" Henry pressed.

"No, it wasn't exactly like that." He gazed up at him mournfully.

"Then how exactly was it? I'm all ears!"

"Adam was the one person who showed me respect, showed me proper friendship. He had my back and I had his every time we went out on that battlefield. We were patrolling at night near the bunkers, keeping an eye out. He said if anything was to happen to him for me to look Molly up and make sure she was alright. To tell her he loved her."

"But he didn't tell you to bloody impersonate him though, did he?"

"No, of course not. I told him I would find her and give her his message. I gave my word. We walked on through a clearing… there were some Jerries quite a way up ahead from us. We crouched down behind a tree for a quick smoke, waiting for them to move further away."

"And then what?" Henry urged, this was all too raw, he too shared painful memories of the war and hated to speak or think about them, but he needed to know more.

"He said," Mathew brushed away a tear and took a deep breath. "He said when your time is up it's up, I'd rather take a bullet outright than to return an invalid. The moment he finished speaking, a gunshot fired at close range and he fell to the ground dead, right in front of me. I checked his pulse, he was gone so I fled like a coward, dodging bullet after bullet, and got back to the bunker safely. It... it should have been me." He cried, rocking back and forth like a small child, with his knees pulled right up to his chin. "I should have stayed put and let them kill me."

Henry reached out, hesitated and then patted his shoulder with a modicum of sympathy. They sat for a while in silence and then Henry said at last, "So why lie and let us all think you were Adam?"

Matthew sighed wearily. "When I arrived at the farm, your mum was so shocked and happy to see me, convinced that I was Adam, fit and well, like some miracle had happened. She rushed off to find your Dad and the rest of the family... well, for a moment I just wanted to experience what it would feel like, to have a family who cared about me, who were actually happy to see me home safe and alive."

"So why didn't you put them straight afterwards? Why go all the way to bloody Scotland and carry on with the charade?" Henry was starting to feel angry again. He just couldn't understand why he would do such a thing, unless... "For financial gain, is that it? To get your hands on my sister's inheritance from our aunt? Fancy yourself lord of the manor, was that it?"

"I had nowhere else to go," he cried pathetically.

"Bollocks!" Henry grabbed him by the throat. "You

could have gone anywhere but there. You were taking advantage of my sister, pretending to be her dead fiancé... you're one sick bastard!"

"Yes I am sick, alright, I'm sick!" he croaked.

Henry released his grip. "Did you even lose your memory, or just your bloody mind?"

"I never meant to hurt anyone." He looked up at Henry with a tearstained face, crying openly again. "Adam was my friend, I didn't want to hurt his girl, his family... I... Look, beat me up, kill me, do whatever you want... I'm done with living now." A sob caught the back of his throat. "I want out, so if you don't finish me off, I'll do it myself... I can't deal with living any longer."

"For Christ's sake man, you need help, serious help." Henry removed his cap and ran his fingers through his thatch of dark curls, anxiously trying to decide what to do with him. He wished he had not met him off the train now, but he had and he felt responsible for him. He couldn't walk away knowing the man was thinking of killing himself, could he? Whatever he had done, Henry knew he couldn't live with another man's death on his conscience. It had been hard enough during the war to do that, but now it would be impossible to live with. But he couldn't take him back to Hazleton Farm, his father wouldn't help save the man's life, he'd most probably kill him himself.

"Look, um... I'm going to take you to Pompey, there's a hospital there that deals with..."

"Mental nutcases like me, yes I know, but if it's all the same, I'd rather not."

"I'm not leaving you here, you need help. My car is parked at the train station. Come on." He pulled Matthew reluctantly to his feet. "They'll be able to advise, put you in contact with the right people about housing, too."

157

Matthew didn't reply, too dejected and not caring what happened next, so he walked on without another word.

Chapter Thirteen

"All I'm saying is, you knew in your heart that Adam was dead, you said so enough times." Daphne placed the blanket she was knitting down and looked over at Molly.

"Yes, until that idiot turned up making me believe he was Adam and that changed everything... he has ruined my memory of the man I loved."

"How? Memories can't be erased, all the good times you had together."

"I feel like a fool, humiliated, thinking of Adam in such a bad way when all the time it wasn't him at all, and poor Adam was in a ditch with other soldiers left to rot, not even a..." she wiped her tears again. She was too upset and wasn't making any sense to Daphne. "Not even a proper grave. And he won't be flown back to England, they only do that with sergeants and corporals and so forth, soldiers of high rankings... He'll be buried over there in France, no doubt and no one to visit his grave."

"You don't know that for sure, you need to contact his parents."

"I can't, they've moved. I wouldn't know how to find them."

"Maybe they're in the phone directory. Look, Molly, what's happened has happened. It's tragic news, I know, and that boy played us for a fool but we've got other things to worry about now, like the wood rot and keeping this place from going under. You need to pull yourself together and focus on that now. I need help, ideas on how to raise the money for it."

Molly stared at her incredulously. "Is that all you care about? How can the wood rot be more important than where my fiancé's body is laid to rest? Are you really so heartless?"

"How dare you?" Daphne responded with resentment. "I'm far from heartless but there comes a time when you need to accept that loved ones die and there's nothing we can do about it. If they'd not found his body, you'd be none the wiser and wouldn't be moping around again. You've already done your grieving for him."

"None the wiser? Done my grieving? I've heard enough." She stood up abruptly knocking her half-finished cup of tea over the coffee table. The brown liquid trickled across the wood and down onto the new red carpet, creating a dark stain.

"Molly, where are you going? We need to sort this."

"There's nothing to sort. I have the money for the wood rot. Vicar Norman and Joan arranged a church fair and we raised the money, it was meant to be a surprise. Not that you deserve it."

Daphne looked at her horrified. "You did what? Over my dead body! I will not accept charity funds. I would rather lose this place than to take money off that imbecile of a vicar and have folk round here pitying me. I can see this has all been a big mistake!"

Molly's eyes gleamed with anger. "Oh yes, it has been a very big mistake!" She stormed out of the room, grabbing her coat and slamming the front door so hard that the old manor house shuddered throughout.

She raced across the courtyard and towards the fields, so angry that she felt like she would explode. It was all too much - finding out about Adam's death, an intruder pretending to be Adam - she still had no idea who he was or why he should do such an awful thing, and what really hurt the most was that Aunt Daphne seemed more

160

bothered about the wood rot than any of it.

"Molly!" Daphne shouted out from the steps. She could see Molly heading deeper into the fields. Exasperated, she called again.

Ross placed the shears down and rushed over to Daphne.

"Oh Ross, thank goodness. Go after her and make sure she doesn't go back to that blessed tree. Tell her she needs to come back here and speak to me properly."

Ross nodded, not understanding what was going on, and sprinted off.

Molly reached the Ghost Tree. Its big branches were wet again from another recent downpour, dripping raindrops beneath it. A crow, startled by her sudden appearance, flapped its wings into the grey sky. She stood for a moment, wondering why she always seemed to come back to the tree - always back to Fergus. It was ironic that her life with him had been full of danger, well, as far as she had witnessed, it had been, yet being with him made her feel safe. When she was with Fergus, Adam didn't exist; it was almost two hundred years before Adam and even Ross were born. Without thinking, she instinctively reached out her hand and touched the inscribed heart. A moment later, she slid down the side of the trunk and sat propped up next to it, rain drops dripping down her face and her eyes staring vacantly ahead, lost once more in the past.

Little Mary was with Nanny, Ian was out collecting rags over the city and Fergus and Michael were at the paper mill, which meant Ella made use of some time alone and headed off to the market. The market square was busy, it was always busy on Fridays and popular with the locals for fresh produce. The carriage dropped Ella off at Fishamble Street as requested, not that she needed to buy fish. The McDaniel's cook had her supplies delivered to Oaklands, but nevertheless, Ella enjoyed meandering to see what was available. One day she hoped that she, Fergus and Ian would be in their own home, preferably on a farm as they had previously discussed, and then she could cook her own freshly grown produce and choose her own fish at the market. She felt sad that they had missed their opportunity at Tullymore Farm. With the outbreak of smallpox and the loss of Clodagh and Lilly, it meant that they weren't able to keep their appointment with Mr Doyle, and even if the old man hadn't yet sold the farm, still it wouldn't be a good time to leave Michael and Mary. They needed family around them and they were all still grieving so much.

Seagulls swooped and dived around the boats coming in and out, their laughing shrills echoing and blending in with the loud banter below, as boxes were being unloaded and new ones stacked on the deck. "I say we show that poster tae a few more locals and then we make our way towards the centre." Jack McKenzie glanced over at Angus, a tall, broad-shouldered young man, eager and ready for the hunt. Ewan nodded in agreement. He was pale, skinny and withdrawn most of the time, but he had more brains than the other two put together, which was why Hamish had sent him. Hamish's small search team consisted of Jack for loyalty - his nephew was blood and he knew he would not let him down - Angus for brawn and his ability to fight well and Ewan was intelligent enough to hunt them down. But if truth be told, whether all three of them lived up to Hamish's expectations or not, they dared not return without a result, each of them fearing for their own lives if they had to tell Hamish they had failed. "I think tae be honest, we'd best head towards the market square," Ewan said, pensively. "I overheard someone say it's the best market of the week, so there's a chance they could be there, or at least the sassenach, anyhow."

"Tae be honest?" Jack mocked. "That'll be a first, you being honest."

Angus smirked at Jack's wisecrack, recalling Ewan stealing weapons from two of the clan members a month ago, and he had been whipped by Hamish and also forced to lick Hamish's boots clean for further punishment.

The trio carried on up the road.

Molly! Ross tapped her face but there was no recognition. He sighed heavily. It could be ages before she woke and he didn't want to leave her, so he sat down next to her and observed her closely, wondering what she was witnessing. Was she back at the same time with the smallpox outbreak or was that all over now? Not being able to resist the urge to find out, he turned and placed his palm on the inscribed heart.

Ella walked on through the fish market and then turned right, heading down a dusty road, dodging carriages as they went in different directions. She could see the market up ahead as she stopped to catch her breath. A short, strong, pain took her breath again as it ripped through her large belly. She'd been having occasional pains these past few days but she still had a couple more weeks to go before the baby was due and she felt sure they were just practising contractions. She contemplated going into Mercer's Hospital. She missed Amelia and the others, and it would be good to get a second opinion about the pains, but she had given her word to Fergus, promised him she would not go back. She was also aware of the fact that young Ian was around town and could easily spot her going in or out of the hospital and she didn't want him to have to lie for her. No, the family had been through enough recently and she wasn't about to cause them more heartache by disobeying Fergus' wishes. She straightened her shoulders and with a stiff upper lip, she walked on.

The sun had been masked behind whispy clouds until she reached the market square. Ella removed her bonnet and wiped her brow, feeling clammy and uncomfortable as she made her way further into the market. Jostled from left to right by the crowds, she stopped to look at a stall of wicker baskets feeling extremely light-headed. She tried to focus on the man shouting out his various prices, but it was no good, she felt too woozy. And then suddenly, her knees caved and she dropped to the ground, knocking her head on a table as she fell. She was out cold.

Jack led the way towards the mayhem at that market. They weaved their way through the masses now gathering. "What's happened?" Angus' big, bushy eyebrows knitted together, as a parting formed in the crowd revealing Ella on the ground, her bonnet half hanging off and her gown covered in mud from the puddle she had fallen into. Jack's beard opened into the widest grin. "Our luck has just come in, that's what's happened."

Ewan pulled out the poster from his coat pocket and checked it, realising what Jack meant - the woman on the ground was indeed Ella.

Jack stood for a moment, noticing her large belly. She was with child. Would Hamish still want her? He shrugged. It was not his decision to make. "Move everyone, dinnae fash, she's family, ma cousin, in fact." He beckoned Angus over to pick her up. Angus, with his large, muscular arms, scooped her up as if she weighed no more than a rag doll. Blood was trickling down the side of Ella's head. A young woman, also pregnant, who had been watching with concern, handed Jack a handkerchief. "Use this to stop the blood."

"Aye of course, but we'll take her somewhere safe first," Jack forced a half-hearted grateful smile and then they left, with Jack leading the way again, Angus in the middle holding Ella, and Ewan trailing behind.

"Take her to Mercer's hospital, it's not far," the woman called out, but her words fell on deaf ears. A moment later the crowd had dispersed and business resumed as usual.

Ian, holding a sack of rags, stopped in his tracks and dropped it to the ground, staring wildly at the scene before him. He recognised Jack McKenzie immediately and then he realised the man in the middle was carrying Ella - they had captured his aunt. He wanted to run after them and shout at them to stop, but he was no fool. There were three of them, all armed and he was an eleven-year-old boy. What chance would he have against them?

Instead, he picked up the sack and followed, keeping out of sight the best he could, needing to know where they were taking her.

"Over there." Ewan pointed to a derelict warehouse; its battered wooden door was slightly ajar. "I'll check if it's empty." They waited while he crossed the small lane and watched him disappear inside. A moment later he appeared, kicking a rat out of the way. "All clear!" he confirmed.

Ian watched them go inside the building and then rushed off to the paper mill to find Fergus, his heart was pounding and his mouth dry from fear. Images of the McKenzies rampaging though Aberdoch Manor were vivid in his mind again – how they slit his uncle's clan members' throats with such ease, like swords gliding through butter. The McKenzies were beasts and he feared terribly for his aunt's life and her unborn child.

Iris walked up the steps of Aberdoch Manor and pounded her fist on the wood of the door before realising there was a bell and then rang it several times. Eventually, Daphne answered looking none too pleased, still vexed at her recent row with Molly and still worried where she might have gone. She eyed the girl up and down suspiciously, wondering if she was a gypsy - maybe a chancer looking to rob the place. She was scruffy enough to be one, in her grubby looking trousers and scuffed boots, nothing lady-like about her.

"Are you Mrs Winters?" Iris asked, having never met her before, although she presumed she probably was

Molly's aunt. She had overheard Norman and Joan mentioning the name Daphne Winters in conversation.

"Who's asking?" Daphne narrowed her eyes further.

"Iris McKenzie." Iris held Daphne's unwavering stare.

"What do you want?" Daphne replied curtly.

"I thought ye might be interested tae know that everyone round here has been working their butt off tae raise money for yer wood rot. God only knows why."

"Firstly, I'm well aware so I don't know why you've come to tell me this. Secondly, I never asked them to raise money for Aberdoch Manor... I'm appalled that they think me to be a charity case. I will not be accepting any money, not a single penny."

"Right." Iris seemed taken aback at her bluntness. It seemed Iris had met her match. "I just thought..."

"Don't think, you're clearly not very good at it. Now go away." Daphne slammed the door then immediately opened it again, taking Iris by surprise. "Did you come through the fields on your way here?"

Iris frowned. "No, I got off the bus from Eyemouth at the main road. Why?"

"Are you walking back through the fields?"

"What's with all the questions, Old Lady?"

"Oi, less of the old, thank you very much. If you see Molly in the fields, tell her she's to come back, we need to speak."

"Tell her your bloody self." Iris retorted, walking away down the steps.

"I would if I didn't have a bad hip... you ill-mannered little..." Daphne slammed the door before finishing her sentence.

Iris smirked and made her way towards the fields. She licked her finger and drew a line in the air. One up for Iris McKenzie!

Ian ran inside the paper mill, dropping the bag of rags just inside the door. He made his way through workers operating machines of all sizes that were hammering and banging, as he crossed the floor to a small office at the back where Michael always sat. He found Fergus going over some papers with Michael.

"Something terrible has happened, you need tae come quick!" Ian blurted out, trying to catch his breath.

Chapter Fourteen

Ella's eyelids slowly opened. She stared at the grey stone ceiling with holes letting in the daylight. She watched a cloud drift past before coming to her senses and wondering where on earth she was. Her head was sore but more than anything it was the pain starting to soar through her stomach that made her cry out, oblivious to the fact that behind her, her capturers were deciding what to do with her.

"Fool! That's a stupid suggestion if ever I've heard one," Jack snarled at Angus in a hushed tone. "What good would she be tae Hamish dead?"

"No tae mention the complications of transporting her body across tae Scotland," Ewan pointed out.

"She's of no use tae him right now is she?" Angus pointed over at Ella rolling on the floor in pain.

"Well obviously no right now no… it looks like the bairn is coming."

"What? Right now?" Both Angus and Ewan watched her in horror.

"Look, what's important is we have her in our possession, which means Fergus will come looking for her. We need tae be ready for him. He's the one Hamish wants dead, not her," Jack said. "We can dump the child at that hospital nearby, get her looking presentable again and take her back wi' us."

Ella heaved herself up and propped her aching back against the cold stone wall. And it was then she saw them, recognising Jack McKenzie standing before her. Her heart pounded in her chest and for a moment she thought she might be sick. "What... what do you want with me? I've done nothing to you. Can't you see I'm having a baby?" Her voice, although wavering, told them she wasn't to be messed with. She looked like a wild animal ready to pounce if they came anywhere near her. A pain ripped at her belly again as she screamed out, forcing them all to move back.

"Alright! Calm down!" Jack shook his head at the other two to stay where they were and not move a step forward. "We want tae help you. Tell me what I need tae do."

"You?" she glared at him with glazed eyes of fear and anger. "You stay well away from me and my baby. I... oh God!" Another contraction came hard and fast, forcing her to scream out again.

Ewan came forward and stood next to Jack. "Shut her up or the whole town will hear."

"And how am I supposed tae do that without harming her?" Jack shook his head with annoyance at him.

Angus walked past them both. "I'll wait outside. I cannae stand back and watch this."

"Good idea, stand watch for Fergus," Jack called out.

"He's hardly going tae turn up any time soon, he doesnae even ken where she is," Ewan said. "In the meantime we are left here delivering his bairn, like a pair of idiots."

"You... You will not be delivering my baby!" Ella simpered, catching her breath before the next contraction. Perspiration was now dripping from her hair and her cheeks were flushed.

"Fergus, wait!" Michael chased after him down the road.

"What?" he stopped for a moment to face Michael. Ian had now caught up with them both. "Ian said they were armed, did you no, lad?"

Ian nodded. "Dirks on their hips."

Michael reached inside of his jacket pocket. "Take this." He handed Fergus a musket. "I keep it at the mill in case of any bandits. It's loaded."

Fergus gave a nod of gratitude then looked over at Ian. "You show me the place from a distance then promise me ye go back tae the mill and stay there until I come for you. I dinnae want ye anywhere near the place, do ye hear me lad?"

"But Uncle, if I come, I…"

"But nothing. Do as I say, lad."

Ian bowed his head reluctantly, then led the way to where he saw the men take Ella.

Angus was bursting, he couldn't hold it any longer. For the moment it was quiet inside, so he dashed down the alleyway at the side of the building and unfastened his trousers as quickly as he could, giving a huge sigh of relief as he emptied his bladder. In mid-flow, he could hear Ella again. *Anyone would think she was being slaughtered.*

Fergus and Michael could hear Ella's screams as they approached the old warehouse. Michael turned to face Ian, scared for the boy and what he might be about to witness. "Now go… back to the mill!" he ordered. With his blood boiling from anger at the McKenzies and fear for Ella's safety, Fergus sprinted across the road and flung back the wooden door, taking it off its hinges as it fell to the ground, forcing Ella to silence from the shock of his entrance. Jack and Ewan backed away nervously, unprepared for Fergus to turn up so soon and pointing a musket gun at them.

"Fergus, what a surprise! We found Ella at the market, she was unwell and so we brought her here. She's having the bairn." Jack did his best to keep calm, wearing a beguiling smile.

Outside, Angus returned to the entrance, noticing the door was now on the floor. He entered. He took Michael from behind, winding him and then punching his face with such strength, forcing him to the floor. Fergus turned around and in a split of a second, Jack had thrust his knife into Fergus' arm as he stumbled from the sudden impact. And taking this opportune moment, Angus grabbed the gun from Fergus' hand.

Ella shuffled her feet, whimpering and trying not to scream and draw more attention to herself. She was terrified for both her own and Fergus' life, not to mention their unborn child's too.

Michael came to and stood up. He joined in the brawl, knocking Ewan out cold on the stone floor before grabbing his dirk. He then cornered Jack, grabbing Jack's knife. And then a single gunshot fired from behind them both. They turned to see Angus still on top of Fergus, blood everywhere.

"Fergus! Fergus! Oh my God, no..." Ella's harrowing cries echoed through the building and into the street outside.

"What the..." Iris stared at them both, wondering if Molly and Ross were dead. She bent down and felt for Molly's pulse. Molly stirred and her eyelids fluttered. They suddenly opened and she let out an agonising cry with the image of the fight and Fergus on the floor with blood everywhere still vivid in her mind. Iris backed away with fright.

Molly felt her stomach, where was the baby? She jumped up searching for signs of blood or the baby on the ground. "The baby! Where's my baby?"

"Mad cow! What the hell is wrong with you?" Iris was clearly freaked by Molly's erratic behaviour.

Molly blinked hard several times before realising she was staring at Iris standing before her. "Iris? What... what are you doing here?" Dazed she glanced over at Ross, who was still under the Ghost Tree's spell.

"Have you two been taking some kind of illegal substance?"

"No, it's nothing like that, I assure you...I can explain..."

"There's something seriously...seriously wrong with you... I cannae..." She was stumbling over her words, edging away from Molly nervously. "I'm getting out of here." Without another word she turned and fled.

"Ross!" Molly tapped his face. His eyes gently opened. He then grabbed his arm against the pain ripping through his flesh.

"Ross, what is it?" She pushed his hand out of the way, pulled back his jacket and lifted his sweater sleeve and then his shirt beneath it revealing his skin. "Look, there's nothing there," she said, trying to reassure him.

"I... Fergus was stabbed," he said, finding his words, realising he was now back in the present again.

"I know, and shot," she added. The haunting scenes suddenly brought back her panic. "Oh God, Ross, I think Fergus was shot dead... that must be how you died." She flung her arms around him and he held her tightly trying to get his head around witnessing his own past death, before realisation set in. "No ye're wrong, I'm sure I wasnae dead. I could feel the weight of him on top of me, I could feel ma knife wound, but no other wound, and if I was dead, I couldnae have felt anything.

They sat for a while without speaking, each of them lost for words and in their own thoughts about what they had just seen. At last Ross spoke. "We really shouldn't do this. It's easier not knowing."

Molly nodded her head in agreement.

"Why did you go back to the tree, Molly?"

"I was upset. Things were getting too much." She sighed and looked at him tearfully. "Adam is dead," she proclaimed.

"Oh, my God, how? I only saw him yesterday morning."

"No, Ross, that wasn't Adam." She pulled out a handkerchief from her pocket and blew her nose.

"Aye, it was, I saw him quite clearly heading up the steps with some planks of wood."

"He was pretending to be Adam."

He watched her with a perplexed expression. "How can he... sorry, Molly but ye've lost me."

"He looked like Adam. He told us he'd had surgery after the war and lost his memory but it wasn't Adam."

"How could you not know he wasn't Adam? I mean, you were engaged to Adam for goodness' sake, Molly."

"Don't look at me that way, I feel an idiot as it is. I wanted to believe it was Adam. My whole family thought it was him. We believed the surgery story, the loss of memory, thinking the war had changed him and then..." she let out a small sob. "And then a telegram arrived at Hazleton Farm. My mother opened it." She looked up at him, distraught. "Adam's body was found in France, in a mass grave."

"Oh, Molly." He took her into his arms and held her close as she cried uncontrollably. Realisation of Adam's death had now set in and the pain tore at her heart.

"Where is he now, the imposter?"

"Gone." She looked up at him, forlorn. "He went early

this morning, took all his stuff before we even knew about Adam's body being found."

"Good, because if I get ma hands on that bastard, I'll kill him."

Michael bent down and rolled Fergus over, revealing Angus beneath him with a gunshot wound straight through his chest. Fergus groaned loudly from the pain in his arm, blood trickled over the floor.

Realising Angus was dead and Ewan still out cold, Jack decided this was the best time to scarper, while all the attention was on Fergus and Angus. He slipped out of the door, colliding with Ian in his haste. "Uncle!" Ian raced into the room.

Michael had torn his shirt and handed it to Ella. Ella, trying her best to conceal her own pain, was relieved to see Fergus wasn't the one who had been shot. She wrapped the material tightly around his arm, applying pressure to stop the bleeding.

They all looked up with surprise and glad to see Ian, even though both Michael and Fergus had told him implicitly to stay away. Ian had acted on impulse. Having returned to the mill, he was too worried to sit and do nothing; he felt the need to try and help.

Ella beckoned him closer, doing her best to control her pain. "Ian, go to Mercer's Hospital and tell Amelia I need her help, tell her my husband is badly wounded and the baby is coming." She let out a harrowing cry as a new contraction ripped through her stomach once again.

"Aye! Aye, of course, right away, Auntie Ella!"

"We should head back or your aunt will have ma guts for garters." Ross stood up and held out his hand for Molly.

She grabbed hold of it. "I wish we didn't have to go... I'll get back and Auntie will be nagging me again, asking where I've been, probably still livid about how I raised the money for the roof."

"She should be grateful that everyone round here wanted tae help. Have you enough money now?"

"I think so. I need to check with Vicar Norman. Although I've no idea how I'm going to pay for the roof if Aunt Daphne won't let me."

"Well if she willnae swallow her pride, the roof will fall down and it will be goodbye Aberdoch Manor... Molly, she has tae accept it if she cannae get the money from another source."

Molly stopped walking. Her lips curled into a small smile. "That's it, another source... Ross you're a genius."

"Aye, I've been called that many times... not," he gave a short laugh.

"All we need to do is get someone else to say they are giving us a loan. I'm quite sure she'd take the money off anyone but Vicar Norman."

"Well, she willnae believe I've got that kind of money," Ross said.

"If I speak to my mum on the phone, when Auntie's not around, and explain... Mum knows how stubborn Aunt Daphne can be and she wouldn't want us to lose the hotel. Oh, Ross... Genius Ross!" She kissed him hard on the lips and then ran off.

"Wait for me!"

"Slow coach!" she called out, glancing back over her shoulder at him.

"I'll give you slow coach, Molly Hazleton." He sprinted after her as she shrieked and giggled, running as fast as she could.

Ross waved goodbye to Molly as she bounced up the steps, feeling much happier than she had earlier. The adrenaline rush of running and being with Ross again had certainly done her the world of good, despite the awful scenes she had witnessed after touching the Ghost Tree, and despite her sadness about Adam's death. It was as if just for that moment in time, all those bad things had gone away, life was normal, better than normal, wonderful, all thanks to Ross. "Auntie!" she called out, hanging up her coat. "I'm sorry that I ran out on you earlier... it's just..." she walked briskly towards the living room. "Oh my God!"

Daphne was strewn full length, face down, on the living room floor and she wasn't moving.

"Auntie!" Molly ran over to her and knelt by her side.

Daphne gave a loud, painful groan as she tried to move.

"What happened? Tell me before you try to move again."

"It's my hip," Daphne croaked, her eyes watering from the pain. "It was hurting so much and it's like it just gave way. I fell and... I think I must have been out of it for a while."

"You need to go to hospital." Molly grabbed a cushion from the sofa and slid it under the side of Daphne's face for comfort. "I'm going to call an ambulance."

"No, just give me a hand to the sofa. An ambulance will take ages, I can't stay here like this any longer."

"Let me get Ross and we can lift you more carefully." Without waiting for a reply, she ran off in search of him.

"Molly!" Daphne moaned into the cushion.

Chapter Fifteen

"Dad said I'm to clean the sheep pen and you are to feed the pigs because he has to go into town," said Henry, picking up a spade hanging on the stone wall.

Emily frowned. Henry didn't seem himself these past few days. "What's up, Henry?"

"I hate cleaning the sheep pen, I hate this bloody farm." He started shovelling hay from the floor.

"I know that, I mean what's really up? You've been a miserable, moody git... more than normal. Have you received more rejection letters from publishers, is that it?"

He gave a half-hearted smile. "Thanks, ye of little faith. Say what you mean, don't hold back. No, it's nothing to do with my writing."

"Well, whatever it is, it's like you're carrying the weight of the world on your shoulders." Emily placed her shovel back up on the wall and turned to face him again.

"Maybe not quite the world, but enough weight to burden me," Henry confessed. He stopped shovelling for a moment and sighed. "Ems, if I tell you something, do you promise not to tell Mum and Dad, especially Dad?"

"Depends. What have you done?" She eyed him suspiciously.

"Then I can't tell you. You need to swear you won't say a word."

She walked closer to him. He obviously needed someone to talk to and if he felt he could confide in her, then she should be a good sister and agree. "Go on, you have my word." She placed her hand on her heart. "I promise not to tell."

"You know the chap pretending to be Adam, well, I met him off the train."

"Why did you do that?"

"Ems, he's really screwed up in the mind. His name is Matthew Hawley, he served with Adam. They were in the same regiment, best of friends apparently. They called him Adam's twin."

"The likeness is certainly uncanny, he fooled us all," Emily said, pensively. "So, he thought when Adam died that he would steel his girlfriend? That was really wrong, on so many levels... he should never have..."

"He's ill, mentally ill. He wanted to kill himself," Henry interrupted.

"I see. Where is he now?"

"I took him to a friend of mine in Pompey, who helps men from the war. I went back to check on him two days ago and he's been admitted to St James' Hospital."

"Gosh. Does Molly know?"

Henry shook his head. "No. Should I tell her?"

"Absolutely. She needs to know, Henry. Knowing that he was ill might soften the blow."

"What if she tells Mum and Dad?" Henry stared back her with worried eyes.

"And so what if she does? You've done nothing to be ashamed of."

"Apart from helping an imposter whose intention was to fleece Molly and Aunt Daphne."

"An imposter who was ill, Henry. I'm not condoning what he did, of course not, but he's obviously sick and didn't know what he was doing. Besides, he left on his own accord, so it does show good character, I suppose...well not exactly good, but you know what I mean."

"Maybe. I wanted to punch his lights out when I met him off the train. I was so angry, I hated him for what he did, but then…" Henry sighed heavily. "Seeing him break down like that in front of me, so weak and so pathetic…"

Emily linked arms with Henry. "You did the right thing. Just pick up the phone and tell Molly."

Henry nodded.

"Right, I better go and feed the pigs." Emily made her way towards the open barn door.

"Ems?"

She turned to face him again.

"Thanks," he said.

She smiled, acknowledging his gratitude before leaving him alone with his thoughts.

The surgeon, young and tall with a thick thatch of dark hair, finished treating Fergus' wound. "You've enough stiches now to stop the bleeding and help the flesh to mend," he said, finishing the dressing.

"Thank you, can I see ma wife now?" There was desperation in Fergus' tone. Surely, the baby was born by now. She had been in a lot of pain in the warehouse and the contractions were coming strong and fast as they left. He felt certain the baby would be born en route to the hospital if they weren't fast enough.

"Not just yet, I'm afraid." He stepped back and looked him in the eyes. "The bairn hasn't arrived yet and she's having a hard time of it, so I'm told. I'll let you know when it's all over and your son or daughter has arrived." He gave a fleeting smile and turned towards the door, then suddenly remembered something. "Your cousin and nephew are still waiting outside. I'll send them in, shall I?"

Fergus nodded, his thoughts still very much on Ella, feeling apprehensive about the surgeon's choice of words - *having a hard time of it.* He couldn't bear it if anything should happen to her or the baby. The thought of living without Ella was too painful to even contemplate and he loved his unborn child already and couldn't wait to meet him or her - his first born, his own flesh and blood.

Michael and Ian entered the room, breaking his train of worried thoughts.

"Uncle!" Ian dashed to his side and perched down next to him on the side of the bed, relieved to see his uncle was looking well despite his anguished expression.

"You were brave, lad. For once I will forgive ye for no doing as ye were told and coming back tae help us." Fergus smiled warmly and the boy grinned, looking pleased with himself.

Fergus glanced up at Michael standing at the foot of the bed. "Any sign of Jack McKenzie?"

Michael shook his head. "No, but we're going tae have tae go back tae the building and dispose of the body before someone sees it. We did well tae hide if from the hospital staff when they arrived."

"Aye, we did." Fergus' eyes clouded. "Michael, ye ken I cannae stay in Ireland now, it's no safe for Ella and the bairn, and neither is it for you or Mary with us being at Oaklands."

"Ye cannae runaway because of *them*. The Red Coats maybe, but those wee…"

"Michael, the McKenzies won't rest until I'm dead." His gaze strayed to Ian's worried face and then back at Michael. "I have a duty tae protect ma family. I've just killed a McKenzie - they'll want revenge and willnae think twice tae…" He stopped in mid-flow not wanting to scare Ian even more than he already had. He knew the lad was in danger, as were all of them. It would only be a matter of time before Hamish McKenzie would be on their trail.

"Where will you go?" Michael rubbed his unshaven chin nervously. He hated to let them go. After losing Clodagh and their unborn child, Fergus, Ella and Ian had been a great comfort to him. It would be lonely without them all.

"I've enough put aside tae fund a passage tae North Carolina. Cousin Finley and his wife, Esme, will make us welcome, I'm sure."

"I dinnae doubt that for a moment, but then what? What are ye going tae live from, money will run out sooner or later?"

"Granted, I dinnae have all the answers just now, but it's the best I can come up with for the time being." There was a tone of annoyance in his voice but his frustration was born out of the situation rather than at Michael's questioning. "First, I need tae get ma family tae safety, then I'll see further."

"Come on Ella, you are doing so well… so you are now… you can't give up, you're doing a grand job. One more push…" Amelia mopped Ella's brow, worried for her. Ella was exhausted and struggled to find even the tiniest amount of strength; she was also losing blood. Her eyes rolled and she was deathly pale. Amelia, realising she couldn't continue this way any longer and needed urgent help, ran as fast as she could out of the room, down the corridor to find one of the surgeons.

The room became bright with a white light, so brilliant that it was blinding as it surrounded Ella with warmth and comfort. She suddenly felt no pain, just peace and serenity. From within the light came a golden glow morphing into the shape of a person. It drifted slowly towards her and she recognised the person standing before her to be Shona, Fergus' sister. She looked peaceful, joyful even, displaying a warm smile. There was a form of communication that took place without words, a sense of just knowing. And then Ella realised this form of communication wasn't in fact coming from Shona, it appeared to be coming from a much higher source, behind her, deeper into the light. It was asking her a question and it was now up to Ella to decide her own fate. Should she continue into the light, or go back?

"Michael, I need tae ken what's happening with Ella. Fergus suddenly possessed a feeling of dread rising from the pit of his stomach, a sixth sense that something terrible had happened. It was a feeling that he could not ignore. He got down from the bed and stood up straight, feeling a little woozy. "We need tae find her, she cannae be far... I must see Ella at once."

Chapter Sixteen

"Your aunt was in a lot of pain and we have heavily sedated her. She has fractured her hip and will need an operation as soon as possible." The doctor sifted through the notes on the clipboard in his hand and then back at Molly and Ross, sitting in front of him in his office. "It should be quite straightforward, no need to worry."

"And how soon can you do it?" Molly asked, hating the thought of Daphne being in so much pain. She knew she had been suffering for a while with hip pain, but she masked it well most of the time.

"First thing tomorrow morning. She'll be in hospital for approximately a week, all going smoothly, but she'll need a lot of support and after care at home. Does she have that?" He asked expectantly.

"Yes, of course."

Ross also nodded. "We will both be there to help. I can help with any heavy lifting."

"Good, because she will need help to get up out of the chair, bed, etc."

"How long is the recovery period?" It was obvious now to Molly that the hotel wouldn't be opening any time soon, even when the wood rot was treated.

"Given her age, about a month, could be less, it just depends on how well her hip recovers from the operation."

"We'll make sure she will get plenty of rest." Ross replied, giving a reassuring smile to both Molly and the doctor, although Molly wasn't convinced that it would be an easy task to get Daphne to rest and she was sure she wouldn't be an easy patient either.

Norman sat on the living room floor with planks of wood and a number of screws and bolts in front of him. He began piecing bits of it together. A moment later Joan could hear his groans and huffing and puffing from the hallway as she slipped her coat on ready to run a few errands for the church. "I don't know why you are building it in the living room. Shouldn't you do it in the shed? Less mess, with all that sawdust.' She buttoned up her coat and carefully slid a headscarf over her neat curls, having gone to the hairdressers that morning.

"There'll be no mess, I've done all the sawing. I just need to put it together and it's better to do it where it is going to be standing rather than struggling to lug it through the house," he called out.

"You know best. I'm off now. Good luck with it all." As she pulled open the door, she jumped to see Molly and Ross standing on the doorstep.

"Sorry, we didn't mean to scare you," said Molly. "I was just about to ring the doorbell."

"Come in." She beckoned them indoors with a friendly smile. "I was just nipping out but Norman is here. Would you like me to make you both a cup of tea before I go?" She checked her watch, she still had a few minutes before she had to meet Maureen and help arrange the new flowers for the church.

"No, it's fine, thank you," Molly smiled.

"We can't stay long," Ross added.

"In that case, let me take your coats and you can go through. I'm sure Norman will welcome the excuse to stop building the new bookshelf for the living room. And if you change your mind, I'm sure he will make you a cup of tea."

"Molly, Ross, nice of you to pop by." Norman's glasses had slid down his nose. He brushed his hands on his trousers as he stood up, before pushing them back up the bridge of his nose again. "Sit down," he gestured towards the sofa.

Molly sat down next to Carrot, who opened an eye, looked disapprovingly at her, then went back to sleep. Ross took a closer look at the wood spread over the carpet. "Joan said you are making a bookshelf."

"For my sins, yes," Norman grimaced. "I'm not a handyman by any means. "I just hope I have cut the pieces correctly."

"Bookshelves are easy enough to make. I'd give you a hand but we need to get back soon…"

"It's fine, Ross, you can stay with Norman and help him. I need to get back but you don't have to. Auntie is in hospital," announced Molly, taking Norman by surprise.

"Goodness. Why?"

"She needs a hip operation. She fell - I found her face down on the living room floor."

"Oh dear." Norman frowned. He had an image in his mind's eye of Daphne sprawled out on the floor, not a pretty sight. He blinked hard trying to erase the image. "If there's anything Joan and I can do… the money, by the way… let me give it to you now."

"Thank you, so much. I need to get the wood rot sorted while Auntie is in hospital. If it's been treated and paid for by the time she comes home, there is nothing she can do about it."

Norman looked confused. "I thought she wanted it sorted?"

"Oh she does, but she's not happy that we raised the money through the church. She feels like she's a charity case, as I predicted she would."

"Oh, so she found out, then?"

"Yes, I told her in the heat of an argument," Molly replied.

Norman pulled a face. "Oh dear, but it is best to be honest."

"It's alright, I've decided that I'm going to tell her that I've not accepted the money and that mum loaned us it instead."

"I think that's a bit dishonest, Molly. You really shouldn't lie to your aunt."

"To keep the peace, I think I should. I need her to rest and not worry about all this. Stress is not good for her and she is going through enough right now."

Norman nodded. As she put it like that, he couldn't deny that Molly's intentions were well meant, even if he didn't agree.

The shrieks of the seagulls were deafening at times as they swooped and dived in and around the boats coming into Dublin harbour. Out of sight, Jack and Ewan stood away from the crowds in a quiet part, taking a moment to contemplate what they had just done. Disposing the body of a dead clan member was bad enough but now they were faced with the impossible task of telling Hamish. The wicker basket they had stolen, laden with Angus' body inside of it with extra stones for further weight, drifted down into the depths of the sea and out of sight

Jack faced Ewan. "What if it washes up somewhere?"

"So what if it does? I doubt it'll be on the shores of Scotland. And if it turns up further down the coastline, the Irish willnae care for a dead Scot."

"Maybe not, but I ken Hamish will." Jack sighed and scratched his matted beard. "I say we have no choice but tae finish the job."

"Aye, ye're probably right but it's no going tae be an easy task with Fergus' impeccable fighting skills and that cousin of his hanging aboot too. Unless ye want tae end up like Angus, I see no choice but tae get help first."

"Jack met his gaze incredulously. Help from where?"

"From back home of course. We can tell Hamish that Angus has been hurt and is in Dublin recovering. It'll buy us some time. He'll assign some more men tae the job."

"And I thought you were meant tae be the brainy one. Firstly, Hamish will be livid tae see us back without Angus no matter what the circumstances are. He wants Fergus' head on a platter and the sassenach as a gift, neither of which we have achieved in case ye havenae noticed. Secondly, by the time we get back tae Scotland and return to Dublin, whose tae say they havenae scarpered, now they ken we are on their trail."

"Aye, ye have a fair point, which is why you should go alone. I'll stay here and keep watch, make sure I ken where they are."

Jack raised his bushy brows. "Me? I'm tae go back alone?"

"Aye, ye're his blood, yer uncle willnae kill you."

Jack contemplated this plan. Although he knew Ewan was probably right that Hamish would likely spare his life, it still didn't stop him from dishing out a heavy punishment, a thrashing of some sort, for having failed the mission he had been given.

"It's the only way out of this mess," Ewan continued.

"For you, maybe," Jack scoffed.

"Well if ye have another idea, I'm all ears. Come on, let's get out of here, I need some food."

*****

Michael and Ian returned to the hospital and found Fergus sitting in a long corridor, alone with his head buried in his hands.

"The body has gone," Michael said in a loud whisper standing in front of Fergus. "The other two must have come back for it."

Fergus looked up with clouded eyes encompassed with dark circles. "I couldnae care less about those idiots just now."

"Any news?" Michael asked, feeling guilty for bothering Fergus at such a difficult time.

Ian placed a comforting hand on Fergus' shoulder. Fergus glanced up and gave a small appreciative pat on his hand. "No," he replied flatly.

The door suddenly opened, taking them all by surprise. Fergus jumped to his feet and rushed towards Amelia. "Is she alright? And the bairn... is the bairn alright?" he demanded.

"I'm so sorry, Mr McDaniel. but your son didn't make it." Amelia did her best to hold back her tears, devastated to be the bearer of such tragic news to her friend's husband.

Fergus stared at her in disbelief. "No, it cannae be so... and Ella?" He held his breath, waiting for her reply.

"She's lost a lot of blood. We've done everything we could, only time will tell now."

Ian let out a small sob and Fergus quickly pulled him into his arms. Fergus swallowed the large lump that had appeared at the back of his throat. "Can I see her?" he croaked.

"It's not advisable. She needs to rest."

Michael placed an arm around Fergus, leading him back to the chair. Michael's own grief was still raw from losing Clodagh and he felt sick from the idea of them possibly losing Ella too.

Chapter Seventeen

Henry had planned to call his sister and explain about Matthew Hawley but she had beat him to it by calling him that afternoon.

"Is Mum there, I should tell her about Aunt Daphne?" She had already filled Henry in with the details.

"She's helping Dad out with the sheep, I think. I can fetch her, but before I do, Molly, there's something I need to tell you."

Molly sat down on the chair behind the desk, the phone still pinned to her ear. "Go on," she said, inwardly grimacing at the cost of the phone call when the bill came in.

"I know who that man pretending to be Adam is. His name is Matthew Hawley, he served with Adam in the same regiment."

"And how would you know that?" Molly's tone was suspicious.

"I met him off the train."

"You did what? Henry…"

"I wanted to give him a piece of my mind, give him what for, for everything he has done, deceiving you and all of us but when we spoke and he explained…"

"Oh don't tell me you fell for his lies too?" Molly sounded dejected.

"No, of course not, but he's ill."

Molly scoffed. "You don't say. Of course he is bloody ill, no one in their right mind would do what he did."

"He's at St James Hospital in Pompey."

Henry had not noticed his mother walking up behind him. "Who's in St James Hospital?" Ruth asked. "And who are you speaking to?"

"Molly's on the phone." Without another word, he thrust the phone into Ruth's hand and dashed off before more questions were asked.

There was a blanket of low grey cloud over the highlands and a light drizzle in the air as Jack made his way towards Dunavard, a sprawling, sandy coloured stone farmhouse, surrounded by acres of land. Hamish, having inherited his parents' home was now not only the head of the McKenzie clan but the family and their estate too. Jack found him in his favourite room, a lavishly decorated sitting room with a bay window looking over the gardens, He was sipping ale and mulling over the rent books handed to him earlier that day by his men who had recently been out collecting from the neighbouring houses and farms.

"Back so soon, I'm impressed." He looked up as Jack entered the room, having seen him walk up the path leading to the entrance of the property. "And how was the Irish connection? I'm presuming the other two are on their way with the sassenach and McDaniel's head on a platter?" His eyes poured over Jack expectantly.

Jack swallowed hard and pushed back his shoulders. "No exactly... you see, we ran into some unforeseen bother."

"What kind of unforeseen bother?" Hamish narrowed his eyes. He rose from his chair, his big frame blocked the daylight from the window behind as he walked towards Jack.

"Angus got stabbed, he's hurt quite badly, ye see. Fergus put up a good fight."

"A good fight?" This was not what Hamish wanted to hear. His patience was already wearing thin. "I didnae care if he did or he didnae, why did you and Ewan not step in? For God sake, how many men does it take to kill one measly McDaniel?"

"The sassenach is with child... we captured her like ye said...tae hold her ransom. That part of the plan worked fine but she started tae have the bairn right there and then on the floor in front of us."

"Christ almighty!" Hamish slammed his fist down on the table. "And then what?"

Jack continued, aware that he must bend the truth a little to save his own skin. "Fergus showed up, a fight broke out as we... well anyway, he stabbed Angus and then some people turned up so we had tae scarper."

"What people?" Hamish's face was becoming redder by the minute.

"I didnae ken exactly who they were but they were making a fuss about the sassenach having a bairn. She was screaming hysterically from the pain ye see... and well, it wasnae the right moment tae finish the job, what with an unwanted audience and..."

Without warning Hamish grabbed Jack by the scruff of his collar, hoisting him up to his own height to face him in the eyes. "Why the hell are ye here? Why are ye no in Dublin planning yer next move?

Jack gulped. "Like I said, we're one man down and Fergus has men there too." He knew it was an exaggeration, Fergus only had one other man at his side but he could have had more. "So I need back up and we didnae ken if you still wanted the sassenach, with her being... well less than desirable, so tae speak..."

He dropped Jack to the floor, and he landed with a thud. He quickly stood up straight, facing Hamish, awaiting his answer, petrified of what he might do next.

"Fool!" he roared. "Ye havenae the brains ye were born with."

"I'm truly sorry, Uncle, I am, but if ye send a couple more men with me, I'll return straight away and finish the job. I'll bring McDaniel's head back for ye on a silver platter even… and if ye still want the sassenach…"

"Shut up!" he roared again. "Ye're no capable of bringing a lump of cheese back on a platter… and as for the sassenach, she's damaged goods, of course I didnae want her now." He scratched his beard and resumed his seat in front of the window, lost in thought.

Jack stood frozen to the spot without saying another word, waiting patiently.

At last, Hamish spoke. "We'll leave at daybreak, tomorrow."

"Ye're coming wi' me?" Jack's tone was one of surprise and concern, wondering how he could keep Angus' death from him once they arrived in Dublin. On second thoughts, as long they didn't let slip of his death, Hamish would presume Angus ran away, perhaps stowed away on a boat to some foreign land, having lost his bottle to finish the mission of killing Fergus McDaniel.

"Aye, if ye want a job done properly ye have tae do it yerself, so it seems." He appeared a little calmer now that he'd had time to process the news. "Dinnae think ye can get away with this, Jack McKenzie. When this is all over, ye'll take yer punishment just the same as any other man who fails to do what I ask of him. There'll be no favours because ye're ma nephew. You'll be flogged in front of the clan just as soon we return, make no mistake."

Jack hung his head with remorse. The only saving grace was that the punishment would be given on their return, which could buy him time, enough perhaps to get back into his uncle's good books.

"Mrs Brady cooked us a potato and leek pie for supper, will you stay?" Molly asked, turning around expectantly, only to find no one was standing behind her. "Ross!" she called out, wiping her hands on a tea towel and then going in search of him. They almost collided as the front door sprung open and he stood before her with arms full of logs.

"I'm just putting some firewood in the front room, I noticed it was getting low," he said, making his way down the hallway. "Did you manage tae speak tae yer mum about the money?" he asked, glancing back over his shoulder at her.

"Yes. Ross, did you come in the kitchen just a minute ago?" She followed him into the living room.

"No, I've been chopping up firewood in the yard, why?"

"I could have sworn someone was standing right behind me when I was at the kitchen sink."

He dropped the logs down beside the fireplace and looked up at her. "Fergus perhaps?" he said wryly, raising an eyebrow.

"That's what I'm wondering, but it doesn't make sense. I've not felt him around since before Christmas and..." She fell pensive.

"Go on..." he stood up straight, brushing wood dust from his hands.

"It's just, like I said before, I don't understand how he

196

could be around in spirit if he's reincarnated into your body. Surely a spirit can't be in two places at the same time?"

"Um… I was reading a book over Christmas on the subject of spirits and life after death. It got me thinking after the whole Ghost Tree experience. It explained that a person can leave an impression in a place that was significant to them in their life… like a blueprint stuck in time."

"I don't follow," Molly frowned.

"I mean, something important happened here, right?"

"Devastating is probably a better choice of word." Molly's thoughts drifted back to the awful 1746 massacre.

"Yes, well, it's like an image that is stuck in time because of a tragedy. It plays over and over again but a ghost has no feelings, no rational thinking. You can't reason or speak with a ghost, but you can with a spirit."

"I still don't understand. What's the difference between a ghost and a spirit?" Molly perched down on the armchair feeling even more confused.

"A ghost is just a replay of an image that is stuck in time, seemingly roaming around but it's just a memory, an impression, whereas a spirit lives on after death and passes over to the spirit world." Ross sat down on the sofa opposite her.

"So don't spirits also roam around a house and show up?"

"I'm not sure but if Fergus' spirit reincarnated and I'm the living proof, then what you felt in the kitchen just now was…"

"The ghost impression of him." Molly concluded, now following his train of thought.

"I don't know for sure, of course, I'm just stabbing in the dark here. Maybe we should ask a medium, they might know." He gave a meek smile.

"I don't think so. All that hocus-pocus gives me the creeps." Molly mockingly shivered.

"Anyway, what did your mum say? Was she alright about saying the money has come from her to fix the roof?" Ross asked, changing the subject. He had to admit, he didn't feel overly comfortable speaking about ghosts and spirits either. He was still trying to get his head around reincarnation; the idea that he had lived two hundred years ago was still difficult to comprehend.

"She said she felt uncomfortable lying but when I explained we would lose Aberdoch Manor if we didn't get this sorted quickly, she agreed. I think her agreeing was more for my benefit to protect my inheritance than anything else. She knows how stubborn Auntie can be at times."

"Great, so that's sorted then."

"Ross... Henry picked up the phone when I called my mum. He told me that he met that imposter, pretending to be Adam, off the train."

"Why? I hope he gave him what he deserved."

"I think he might have given him a hiding, Henry was very upset about the whole thing, but he said this chap's name is Matthew Hawley and he served with Adam, and that he is mentally ill. He's now in a mental hospital in Portsmouth."

"Right, well, yes, obviously he is ill to pretend to be someone he's not. I mean, who in their right mind would do that?"

"Yes, I know." Molly shivered, thinking about him. Can you stay for dinner? It's potato and leek pie," she said, changing the subject. She didn't want to think about him for a moment longer, she had to put the whole sorry experience behind her or she feared for her own sanity.

"Try stopping me. His expression turned to one of

concern again. "Molly, I don't want you to take this the wrong way, but I was wondering, what with your aunt being in hospital and you being all alone in this big old house, could I stay, just until she comes home? In a spare room of course," he quickly added, not wishing her to think him being forward.

She walked over to him and sat down next to him of the sofa. "You really are the most thoughtful man I've ever met. Yes, I'd love you to stay." She placed a kiss on his lips. "I love you Ross McDaniel."

"Just as well because I'm nuts about you!" He smiled broadly.

Chapter Eighteen

"Ella, please wake up!" Fergus held her hand tightly. Michael waited outside of the room with Ian. Against the doctor's wishes, Amelia had insisted that Fergus should sit with Ella, especially as it was unknown if she would ever wake up again. She seemed even smaller than he remembered, laid in bed with her fair hair sprawled out over the pillow and her face deathly pale and withdrawn.

"I cannae live without ye," he sobbed, bringing her limp hand to his lips. "I cannae be without ye, Ella, ma *leannan*, please wake up!"

Ross' eyelids fluttered in the dark bedroom. A small shine of silver light from the moon outside filtered in, casting a glow over the foot of the bed. Keeping true to his word, he had taken the smallest bedroom in the left wing of the property. His head turned from side to side, restless as tears rolled from beneath his eyelids, trickling down his face.

Ella's head slowly tilted to one side and he could feel her

fingers move in the palm of his hand. "Ella!"

Her eyes softly opened and she stared at him, confused and dazed.

"Ye're alive, oh thank the Lord. I'll be forever in His debt."

Her eyes then closed again and her head rolled back into the same position as before.

"Ella! No! Ye cannae leave me… no!"

"No, dinnae leave me!" Ross shouted out into the darkness, sitting bolt upright and gasping for breath. He blinked several times but the images were still there in his mind. He rushed to the window and opened it. The cold night air hit him instantly, stinging his face. Had he just witnessed Ella's death? But how? He wasn't even at the Ghost Tree. Then it dawned on him. This was the first time he had slept at Aberdoch Manor and somehow it was stirring up past life memories. He shivered and closed the window, then got back into bed under the covers, too scared to go back to sleep. He doubted he could sleep even if he wanted to, after what he had just seen.

The sky was a bright blue and the air crisp as Molly and Ross made their way inside Eyemouth hospital. Ross had decided not to tell Molly about his dream, or whatever it might have been, it wasn't fair for her to know how she (Ella) had supposedly died. He contemplated if he himself would have liked to have known for sure how Fergus had died. But all thoughts of this were pushed aside as they arrived at the reception desk and were soon greeted by the surgeon, wearing a cheerful smile. "All went well, I'm pleased to say, the procedure was straightforward, as expected. Your aunt seemed to have a relatively peaceful night, so the nurses on duty have told me. We'll be keeping her in for about five to seven days and all being well, you'll be able to take her home to continue her recuperation."

"That's wonderful news. Can we see her?" Molly asked, relieved that the operation had been a success.

"Of course, she's allowed visitors now. Nurse, would you…" He pointed to a young nurse not much older than Molly. She smiled obligingly and led the way.

"Ah, there you are, you took your time. Did you bring those magazines I asked you to fetch from the living room?" Daphne sat propped up against several plump pillows, wearing a pastel blue nightdress and a pink crocheted bedjacket for warmth around her shoulders.

"Yes, I did. Good to see you, Auntie." Molly kissed her on the cheek and pulled out the magazines from the bag hanging over her shoulder.

Daphne's pale face lit up. "Ah good, there's a couple of crossword puzzles I've not finished in these." She flicked through, searching for them.

"Hello, Mrs Winters. How are ye feeling now?" Ross stood at the foot of the bed.

"Eh… what?" She looked up at Ross, distracted by the magazines.

He raised his voice. "I said, how are you feeling?"

"I'm not deaf, no need to shout. If you must know, sore, to say the least, but the last lot of painkillers the nurse gave me at breakfast are starting to kick in now. Molly…" She placed the magazines to one side and looked at her. "I need to speak to you… alone, if we may."

Molly glanced over at Ross apologetically.

"It's fine, I'll go and see if I can rustle up some tea for us somewhere." Ross left the room.

"I've… well, I've made a decision… You'd best sit down." Daphne pointed to the chair and Molly sat, not liking the sound of her tone.

"Having that fall and the need of an operation has helped me to realise that I'm not as fit as I thought I was after all."

"Well, once your hip is healed you'll be as good as new. You're in good health other than your hip," Molly said, with an encouraging smile.

"I'm seventy, Molly. What was I thinking, starting a hotel at my age? I don't want to be running around after guests, I should be retired, not starting work again."

"But you won't be working. You have me and staff to do it all, you just oversee everything, and you don't even have to do that if you don't want to. I'll take care of it all if you'll let me," Molly pointed out, trying to reassure her further. She couldn't lose the hotel, not now, it was her home and it was her future. There was no way Molly wanted to go back to her old life at Hazleton Farm.

"Look, Molly, it's my fault. I gave you the idea of running a hotel but I can't be a part of it any more. I'm not going to leave you high and dry, though. I'll make sure you'll get your inheritance, but I'm going to sell the place."

"But what about the wood rot, you can't sell it in the state it's in," Molly said, omitting to tell her that workmen were about to start on it tomorrow morning. "And you didn't want to accept the church money, remember?"

"I've thought about that too. The money has been given to me, and will come in handy. What is it they say?

Never look a gift horse in the mouth. Besides, when I move, I'll never have to see that vicar and his wife again, so I won't need to feel like a charity case, will I?"

"They don't think you are a charity case, Auntie. Vicar Norman and Joan are decent caring people, they only wanted to help."

Daphne licked her dry lips. "Well, anyway," she said, continuing with the conversation. "We'll take the money, get it repaired and then I'll put the property back on the market. When it is sold, I'm going to give you a percentage of the sale money. It's your inheritance so you don't have to wait for me to pop my clogs to get all of it, although I doubt you'd need to wait too long now anyway, but you'll get twenty-five percent immediately, so you can start another business if you want and the rest will come to you when I finally kick the bucket."

"Auntie, stop this talk! You are not going to die for a very long time and I don't want another business or for you to sell Aberdoch Manor. You can't - too much work has been put into it already..."

"Which is a good thing," Daphne intercepted, it will increase the value and with the wood rot treated, I'll get a reasonable price. Now listen, Molly..." She sat forward and winced from a shooting pain rising in her hip and making its way down the side of her leg. "Like I said, with the money you'll get, you can start another business and I'll help you decide what. Granted, it won't be a hotel the size of Aberdoch Manor, but you might be able to get a guesthouse if your heart is set on being a hotelier one day."

"But I don't want a guesthouse, I want Aberdoch Manor." She sounded like a small child about to throw a tantrum as her bottom lip quivered and tears sprang to her eyes.

"Well, I'm sorry, Molly, but I've made up my mind.

I'm going to buy myself a little cottage in the countryside and get myself a small dog. That's all the excitement I need in life and you can do whatever you want with your share, you and Ross together. Like it or lump it!"

Molly was too upset to listen to any more, and dashed out of the room, meeting Ross as he came down the corridor holding two plastic cups of tea.

"Put them down, we're going," Molly said, wiping her tears with a handkerchief she had found in her coat pocket.

"What? Why?" Ross ran after her, bemused.

Chapter Nineteen

"The baby?" Ella looked at him in panic, now awake and feeling a little stronger but terrified of his reply. Her head was throbbing and her whole body ached from head to toe. She struggled to remember the birth. Only flashes of her pushing, crying from the pain and then feeling dreadfully weak came to her sporadically, but she couldn't recall the baby arriving or her holding it in her arms. Tears sprung to her eyes. "Where's my baby?" she cried.

His expression was full of sorrow. The pain etched all over his face, gave her the answer she had dreaded, but still she needed to hear Fergus say the words for fear that she would never believe him. "Where's my baby?" she whimpered pathetically.

"I'm so sorry, Ella, they couldnae save him, it was a boy."

She let out a pitiful wail. He moved closer and took her into his arms, holding her tightly as she cried. Her shoulders shook from the pain and the grief that they both now had to bear. A pain so great that it ripped at their hearts and would leave yet another undeniable hole in their lives forever.

A white van pulled away, its tyres crunched on the gravel as it made its way along the lane and under the grey stone archway. Molly flopped down on the front door step and sighed heavily. She felt like she could just sit and cry, if only she had the strength. Ross sat down next to her. "Why the glum face? I thought you'd be pleased, the workmen have gone, the wood rot is finally fixed."

"I am, but what's the point if Aberdoch Manor is going to be sold? And on top of us losing our new home and business, I received this earlier today." She pulled out a letter from the side pocket of her dungarees.

"Who's it from?" Ross frowned.

"Adam's mother. It was sent to Hazleton Farm and mum didn't open it, she just sent it with other post to me."

"I presume we are speaking about the real Adam's mother?" Ross asked, to be sure.

"Yes, of course," she replied with a hint of annoyance. "It was an invitation to a memorial service for Adam, held yesterday at St Mary's church in Portsmouth."

"Oh," Ross grimaced. "And ye only received the letter this morning. I'm sorry Molly, I really am."

She sighed again with regret. "I probably wouldn't have gone, anyway."

"Why not?"

"How could I have left this place with Auntie in hospital, me supervising the workmen and getting everything ready for the opening, which of course is a waste of time now?"

"I could have managed for a few days."

"There would have been no point in me going." She blinked hard against the tears brimming her eyes. "I would have felt… it would have felt wrong to sit there with his family, grieving when I have a new life now in Scotland with you."

"It's not wrong to move on, Molly, you thought he

was dead, and he is. You are young, you are entitled to have a new life. Unless of course you don't want a new life with me anymore?" He held his breath, waiting for her reply. He could not bear it if she said she didn't want him now. They were meant to be together; a life without Molly seemed impossible to imagine.

"Of course I do, silly." She bumped shoulders with him and smiled meekly. "It's just I blame myself... maybe I should have waited until I knew for sure that he was not ever coming back or that he had definitely been killed, before I started a new life without him, here in Scotland." She wiped a stray tear away from the side of her nose.

"You weren't tae know they were going tae find his body. You cannae be expected tae sit and wait in hope forever. And tae be fair, when ye thought that chap... the one who pretended tae be Adam... was really Adam, and that he was back for good, you were willing tae sacrifice what we had to be with him. You showed yer loyalty then."

"Not really. I was planning on calling off the engagement, all I wanted was to be with you."

"Because he wasnae the real Adam. I bet if he was, ye wouldnae have wanted me. He would have come back and swept ye off yer feet. I'm not stupid, Molly. He was the love of yer life, ye were engaged tae the man."

Molly stood up. "Well it doesn't matter now, does it? Adam has gone and he won't be coming back. I missed the service and that's that." She brushed passed Ross and went indoors.

Norman hung his coat up on the peg, slipped out of his shoes and padded into the living room. "Hello, Love, I'm home," he called out, but the only reply he got was from

Carrot, who gave a disconcerted squeak of a meow from the armchair and then went back to sleep. "Joan!" he called out again, heading towards the kitchen, but before he arrived there, passing through the hallway the front door opened and in she walked.

"Oh, Norman, take this shopping bag, it weighs a ton." She handed it to him and then hung her coat up.

Norman took the bag into the kitchen.

"You're home earlier than I expected," she said, slipping her feet into a worn out pair of comfortable, green slippers. "Did you get my note I left on the kitchen side?"

"I have now," he said, his voice echoing from the kitchen. He read the note explaining that she had got delayed earlier with Molly coming round and she still had to pop to the shop and dinner would be later than normal.

"What did Molly want?" Norman asked, taking a seat at the kitchen table. "Does she need any help at Aberdoch Manor? I never thought - we really should have popped over there."

"That's what I thought when she arrived, we've been so busy though, haven't we?" She sighed wearily and then started putting the shopping away. "It was about the opening of the hotel."

"Oh, do they have a date? What about the wood rot, is it sorted now?"

"Yes, to both your questions. She's set a date for the first of March."

"That's only four weeks away, will they be ready by then, I mean Daphne too?" Norman asked with surprise, aware that Daphne was still in hospital.

"Well, the wood rot has been treated, but you will never believe this..." She turned to face him. "Mrs Winters wants to sell the place and so Molly and Ross have worked tirelessly this past week to get it ready to show her that it is a viable business after all, hence the setting of the opening date so soon. I think they would have done it even sooner if it wasn't for the fact that Daphne needs some recuperation time."

Norman's eyebrows knitted together. "But I don't understand, why does Daphne Winters want to sell up all of a sudden? Regardless of whether she thinks the money has come from the church or not, the wood rot is now fixed, so what's the problem?"

"Well, she doesn't know yet that it is fixed, but she did tell Molly that she was willing to use the money raised by the church, so at least Molly didn't have to lie about it… I'll put the kettle on." Joan grabbed the kettle from the stove and filled it up from the tap. "I think," she raised her voice over the noise of the water gushing out of the tap, "the fall she had and her hip operation has brought home her age."

"Well, I've always thought it a big project to take on at her time of life but she does have people to help her; Molly for one, Ross, a cook, cleaners."

Joan lit the stove and then sat down at the table for a moment, taking the weight off her feet. "Poor Molly was very upset at the prospect of losing Aberdoch Manor. Mrs Winters had promised to leave it to her in her will you see. Molly has been through so much, what with this terrible business to do with her fiancé."

"Yes, shocking. I still can't believe someone would do such a wicked thing… to pretend like that… so deceitful. Anyway, you know what I think of Daphne Winters but still I would be sad to see them go and the place left empty again. Something had to become of that old mansion and a hotel seems like a good idea."

"You've changed your tune. You weren't exactly for the idea when they first arrived." She raised an eyebrow at him.

"Well, that was when I found out about the 1746 massacre but now…"

The whistle from the kettle cut in and Joan got up to rescue it.

"Anyway, what can we do to help Molly?" he said when the kettle stopped its whistling.

"I think we should offer some help for the opening, at least. I could do some baking. Molly said if the weather is fine, then we could have some tables and chairs outside in the grounds."

Norman chuckled. "Molly is from Hampshire, unaware still of our constant bad weather up here. What are the chances of the weather being fine here on the first of March? It could be snowing a blizzard if it's not pouring with rain or howling a forceful wind."

"You really can be the voice of doom and gloom at times, Norman Fisher. And, if it is bad weather, then it won't matter because most people will be inside looking around the hotel." She handed him a mug of tea. "Shall we go in the living room and we can light the fire, it's chilly in here."

"Alright. What time is dinner? I'm getting peckish."

"I'll have my tea and then crack on with it. I've got some shepherd's pie left over from Tuesday, it'll still be alright if I heat it up and make some fresh gravy. Here…" She grabbed the biscuit tin and handed it to him. "Have one, but don't spoil your tea."

A small ray of sunlight filtered in through a tiny window on the far side of the room, reaching the foot of the bed, casting a long strip of golden glow over the sheet covering Ella's legs.

Fergus sat perched on the side of the bed, holding her hand. "Ella, as soon as ye're well enough, we need tae leave. It's no safe for us tae stay in Ireland anymore."

Ella looked at Fergus, forlorn and broken. "I've no more fight left in me, Fergus. What is the point? Why should we keep on running?"

"Every point and if no for ourselves but for young Ian, at least. He needs us… I promised Shona when I laid her tae rest." He wiped a tear away with his free hand.

"You promised to keep Lilly safe too but I saw to it that you didn't. I'm responsible for two children's deaths," she said, mournfully. "I'm not fit to look after Ian, I'm not fit to be any kind of mother to him," she cried.

"Now you stop that at once! Ye cannae speak like that, do ye hear me?" He took both her hands into his own and looked deep into her eyes. "Lilly's death was no yer fault; ye did yer best tae save her, I ken that now, and neither did ye have anything tae do with our bairn losing its life. God called them both back home and there's nothing we could have done tae stop that."

The door creaked opened and Michael signalled for Fergus to come and speak with him. Ella laid back on the pillow behind her, too blinded from her sorrow to even notice Michael or care what he had to say to Fergus in private.

"How is she?" Michael gazed over at Ella then back at Fergus. Fergus ushered him outside of the room.

"She's no in a good way… in her mind, I mean. Her body is healing well, so I'm told." He glanced down the hallway. "Where's Ian?"

"I've left him at the mill. It's good tae keep the lad busy."

"Aye, it is that, but when he steps out of the mill,

promise me you'll no let him out of yer sight. I've no idea when the McKenzies are going tae strike again."

"Aye, of course. They'll no try anything at the mill, there's too many people around who would see them off in a flash," Michael said. "Anyway, what's yer plan?"

"Tae leave as soon as Ella is strong enough; get a boat tae the Americas. I'll write tae Cousin Finley and Esme this evening."

There was sadness in Michael's eyes, he hated to see them leave. With Clodagh now gone, he and Mary would be alone with no other family around, and the idea of being a single father was somewhat daunting, even with Nanny taking care of Mary during the day. He would miss Fergus, Ella and Ian, he had grown fond of them all these past few months. "Are ye sure ye must leave? I can gather enough men tae help protect our home until we've seen the McKenzies off, good and proper."

"It's no just the McKenzies. If word gets tae the Red Coats Ella is here… and I wouldnae put it past that wee bastard Jack McKenzie tae tip them off… then this becomes far bigger than a clan McKenzie problem."

"I never thought about that," Michael admitted.

"Ian has seen enough bad in his short lifetime and I cannae have him waiting around these parts with so much danger lurking, no tae mention Ella. She's been tae hell and back with everything that's gone on. She blames herself for Lilly's and Clodagh's death still, and now the bairn's too." Fergus' voice broke as he stifled a sob at the back of his throat. Michael reached out and hugged him tightly. "It's going tae be alright, Cousin, it's going tae be alright."

Chapter Twenty

Five members of the McKenzie clan including Hamish and Jack disembarked a boat from Scotland and stood on dry land, watching the chaos of people dashing around in all directions, scrambling to collect their luggage and be on their way as quickly as possible.

"What's yer plan, Uncle?" Jack shielded his eyes against a ray of afternoon sunshine poking through an agglomeration of grey clouds.

Hamish stroked his long matted beard in thought. "We head tae the centre, find ourselves somewhere tae sleep for the night. We can already start frequenting the local taverns this evening tae put the feelers out. I could murder an ale!"

"Is it wise that they ken we are here?" asked Jack. "They may make a run for it."

"How else are we going tae find them if we dinnae ask the locals?" Hamish gave him a sideways glance of annoyance and marched on, shoving his way through the crowds. His men, too scared to offer an opinion of their own, followed suit. Unlike Hamish, who wore his traditional Scottish attire, the others dressed down for the occasion, wishing to look less conspicuous in busy Dublin.

"Are you comfortable enough, Auntie?" Molly stepped back to look at Daphne, sitting in her chair with a plump cushion behind her head for extra support and a brightly knitted patchwork blanket that Daphne had made herself draped over her knees. There was a small round table at the side of the chair with a cup of tea, a generous slice of freshly made carrot cake, and some magazines. Molly omitted to tell Daphne the cake had been baked by Joan, or she wouldn't have eaten it, stubborn as Daphne was, no matter how delicious it looked. Anything that came from the vicarage would be thrown in the bin without hesitation. Molly had thanked Joan that morning before going to collect Daphne from the hospital and then told her Mrs Brady had made it.

"I'm fine. I don't want you to keep fussing." She screwed her eyes up suspiciously at Molly. "Or are you just buttering me up? Do you have something to tell me, is that it?"

"Buttering you up?" Molly echoed incredulously. "Believe it or not, I care about you, even if you are going to sell this place." She sat down on the sofa, her expression awash with disappointment.

"And there we have it, just as I thought…" Daphne pursed her lips.

"Auntie, that's grossly unfair, and I think you are being unreasonable about Aberdoch Manor. You can see how well Ross and I have done to get it in shape, and I'm willing to work as hard as it takes and you wouldn't have to lift a finger… and also…"

"Molly, that's enough. I said I'm selling and that's that."

The loud intrusive ring of the telephone made Daphne nearly jump out of her skin as it rang on the sideboard next to the window. "What in heaven's name?" She turned her head in the direction of the ringing. "Molly, why is there a telephone in the living room?"

Molly got up off the sofa and walked towards it. "I had an extension put in to make your life easier, so you wouldn't have to walk down the hall to answer it if I wasn't nearby. Another example of how much I care and how efficient I am."

Daphne rolled her eyes.

"Oh, hello, Mum. Yes all is fine, Aunt Daphne is home now."

Daphne sighed heavily. That was the last thing she needed, to talk to Ruth, all she wanted was to drink her tea, eat some cake and get on with a good crossword puzzle.

"Yes, I'll pass you over to her." Molly handed the phone to Daphne.

Daphne took it reluctantly. She forced a smile down the phone. "Hello, Ruth."

The air was cold and damp after a recent heavy downpour over Dublin city. Inside a dimly lit tavern, jovial, loud voices echoed outside and down the wet cobbled backstreets. The tavern played host to quite a few of Dublin's unsavoury characters sitting at various tables - some singing along to a middle-aged, plump woman hammering the keys of a piano, others gambling, engrossed in a game of cards, while a few women with cleavage aplenty and dressed to please served the men drinks, hoping to earn some extra money that night if any of them should take their pick.

Hamish grinned as he ushered his men to a table in the

far corner. This was just the type of place he enjoyed, and he felt very much at home. One of the women made a beeline for the McKenzies, newcomers were always welcome, especially from a different land and hopefully with money.

"What can I get you?" Her tone matched her suggestive hazel eyes. The lines around them and also her lips, showed signs of ageing.

"We'll start with ale." Hamish grinned again, revealing a few black teeth through his thick beard. "And then we'll see what else ye can give me."

She nodded with a look of hope, and as she turned, he slapped her plump backside. She turned to face him again, far from annoyed, in fact, she seemed to enjoy it. "If you want to slap my behind naked, I'm sure it can be arranged." She raised her eyebrows invitingly and he let out a raucous laugh. A few minutes later she returned with tankards of ale on a tray and placed them in the centre of the table.

Hamish's eyes were drawn to her large bosom as she leaned purposely over him. "What's yer name?" he asked, before he took a gulp of his drink, enjoying the fresh coolness.

"Grace," she replied, turning to face him.

"Well then, Grace, you can Grace me with some pleasure." He pulled her towards him and buried his face into her breasts, while she shrieked with excitement." Jack shook his head and the others didn't know where to look, pink faced and sheepish, they quietly sipped their drinks.

The singing became louder. One of the women got up onto a long table, lifting her dress to her knees, she stomped her feet on the wood as they jeered and begged her to come down and give them more. They shoved notes in between her breasts whenever she bent down towards them, securing their place with her later that evening.

Hamish pulled Grace to his lap with force, sliding a hand under her skirts. He quivered from the thrill of her naked skin, becoming instantly aroused.

"Let's go somewhere more private," she whispered in his ear.

Jack watched Hamish take her hand and pat his sporran with a promise of good payment, before she led him off up the wooden staircase above the bar. Hamish would probably not be seen again until sunrise. Unlike his uncle, Jack would rather not waste money on a woman, instead he ordered another drink and got back to the loud banter with the others.

The ticking of the clock on the wall and the clinking of cutlery was almost deafening in the silence of the dinning-room at Oaklands. Ella, still looking pale and withdrawn, pushed a potato around her plate before finally cutting it and attempting to eat. Michael and Fergus had spoken briefly about the mill, new orders that had just come in, and about a large client who was threatening to leave and go to their competitor due to a better offer. But everything, even that which would have been immensely important at one time, seemed so trivial in the grand scheme of things. Michael failed to find the right words to comfort Fergus and Ella, and Fergus was too preoccupied with his own thoughts about leaving. Ian had eaten earlier with little Mary to keep her company and was now in bed, exhausted after a hard day's work at the mill.

Ella patted either side of her mouth with a linen napkin, then stood up. "Please excuse me, I need to rest." She left the room without another word.

Now that she was out of earshot, Michael felt that he could speak more freely and there was something bothering him. "Cousin, I overheard Bill and Eamon, two of the millers, speaking about some Scots arriving in Dublin earlier today. They spotted them in the market square during their break. Eamon asked me if I had relatives come tae stay. He described one of the men as a monster of a man, very tall and big built. Do ye think…"

"Do I think? Aye, of course I think it's them - who else would it be?" Fergus replied, his eyes full of concern and anger. "Why did ye wait so long tae tell me?"

"I only found out before I left the mill and ye had already gone on without me."

"I left early because I wanted tae check on Ella."

"Aye, I ken that and when I got home, Ella was around and I didnae want tae frighten her, what with…"

"Alright, it's no yer fault, I appreciate ye thinking of Ella but we need tae leave on the first boat that sets sail at sunrise." He downed his brandy, slammed the glass down and left the room in haste.

Daphne had polished off the slice of cake and had fallen asleep while working on a crossword puzzle; the painkillers had knocked her out again. Molly removed the magazine and placed it on the table by the side of her before pulling the blanket a little higher to keep her warm. She then picked up the plate and Daphne's finished cup of tea and took it to the kitchen. She struggled to hold back her tears as she left the kitchen and headed for her coat and boots by the front door. She couldn't bear the thought of leaving Aberdoch Manor; it was not only her new home and a future business, but it was also her heritage. The property had belonged to Fergus, she had been his wife once, a very long time ago and for Ross, this was of course more his heritage even than her own. She loved Ross and still ached for Fergus, it was like loving two men at the same time, yet spiritually they were one. Ross deserved to be a part of the hotel just as much as she did. They needed to run it together as a couple; as husband and wife, one day.

She closed the door softly then made her way towards the fields. She couldn't see Ross; he must have been working at the back of the property. The air was crisp as the sun drifted in and out of grey clouds, mounting quite heavily above the hills in the distance. She wiped her tears, thinking about Fergus, the life she had once shared with him. Not able to control her longing to go back to her old life, she found herself standing before the Ghost Tree, staring at the inscribed heart with the initials E&F. She reached out and touched it.

It was still dark as the carriage pulled away and the sound of horses' hooves on cobbled stones drifted into the distance. Fergus, Ella and Ian sat huddled together against the early morning chill with all their worldly goods, which consisted of very little. They had travelled light from Scotland, having had to flee Aberdoch Manor in a hurry and they had not accumulated much in the way of possessions during their stay in Dublin, other than a few more items of clothing.

Michael, damp eyed and full of concern, turned around and went back indoors. Fergus had insisted they go alone; he wanted no fuss to be made about their departure, no big farewell, which would have made it more difficult than it already was. All he wanted was to slip away as quietly as possible by sunrise. Saying goodbye to Michael was extremely painful, especially given all that they had been through together during their short stay. It also felt like a final goodbye to Clodagh and little Lilly, especially leaving Lilly behind. Mary had been asleep and regrettably they were unable to say goodbye to her, although Ian left a note for Michael to read her, saying he would never forget his little cousin.

Dawn was starting to break as they arrived at Dublin harbour. It was already a hive of activity. A ship had just docked carrying passengers from Portsmouth. It was destined for Brest before making its way further south loaded with various cargo. Alongside it were more ships preparing to leave soon.

"Ella, wait there with Ian, I'll check where these ones are heading." Fergus pointed to a row of different sized vessels lined up with crew on board and passengers starting to embark, handing over their hard earned coin. And depending on their wealth it would determine the quality of comfort they would be travelling in.

"We might strike lucky and find one heading straight to the Americas," Fergus added, placing a small wooden trunk by her feet.

She nodded and pulled Ian closer as they stood with their backs to the wall, so as not to get jostled from side to side as everyone dashed about their business. She still looked pasty and unwell. She had passed the point of crying, left only with a feeling of emptiness, a longing for her unborn child and guilt for the deaths of Lilly and

Clodagh.

Ella watched Fergus in the distance, haggling with the captain of a large ship. It was Ian who spotted them first, recognising the small one with a scraggy beard and robust face. He froze on the spot, wondering what he should do. Should he tell his Aunt Ella; he was very much aware of her fragility. But if he was to run to Fergus and leave her alone, he feared for her safety. In the end, he decided the best plan of action was for them both to leave. "We must go tae Uncle Fergus," he said, trying to contain his fear.

"No, we must stay here," Ella replied indignantly, still watching Fergus in the distance.

"It'll be far easier if we go tae him, it looks like he is paying for our passage." Ian pressed, this time with more urgency. "We can get settled on board quicker and less chance of us being seen if we go now."

She dragged her attention back to Ian with a deep frown, but then caught sight of Hamish heading their way. She let out a small shriek of horror. Ian turned his head, following her gaze and it was then that Hamish laid eyes on them both. They instinctively picked up the luggage, Ian taking the wooden trunk and Ella picking up the bags and they ran, darting in and out of the crowds. Hamish, being so tall, could follow them easily; his men were also on their trail, each wanting to be the first one to capture Fergus and get into Hamish's good books - Jack, especially, as it meant he might be pardoned from his promised thrashing. He sprinted on through the crowds, shoving people out of the way with annoyance.

"The McKenzies!" Ella shouted as she approached the ship. Fergus, thrust a bag of coins into the captain's hand and grabbed the luggage from her, ushering her down the steps to the lower deck, praying they had not seen them board. Another crowd entered the deck right behind Fergus, he grabbed Ella and hid behind them. They crouched down behind a stack of chests, taking a moment to catch their breath.

"Where's Ian?" Fergus asked, sneaking a peek over the top of the chests, but there were far too many people for him to see the boy.

Ella rested against one of the trunks, still gaining her breath. "He was right behind me, he couldn't have gone far."

"Aye, he'll be here somewhere. When we set sail, we can look for him."

"What if the McKenzies are on board?" she asked, still with fear in her eyes.

"I'm quite sure they didnae see us. If they were here we'd have heard Hamish's loud roar by now, ye ken what he's like, he doesnae do anything quietly."

Ella shivered at the thought of the beast of a man.

"Which ship did they board, lad? I'll no ask ye again." Jack pinned Ian up against the wall, the damp cold stone rubbed against his head. Hamish and the others were now heading their way.

"That one." Ian pointed to another ship two down from the one Ella and Fergus had boarded.

"The lad said they're on that one." Jack announced, as Hamish and the others gathered around panting and gasping for air.

"What are ye wating for then?" Hamish gave Jack a forceful shove to start running again. Ian, still clutching hold of the luggage, threw it at Jack's face. The small wooden trunk, caught the corner of Jack's eye, releasing his grip on him. Ian grabbed the opportunity and ran as fast as he could before the others had the chance to catch him, dipping in and out of the crowds before finally jumping on board of a ship and hiding behind a large lady who was busy paying her fare. All he needed to do now was wait and let them pass by, and then he could run back in the opposite direction and find the ship his aunt and uncle were on.

"We're moving!" Ella exclaimed with relief. "Where is it heading?" She rubbed her tired forehead, all she wanted to do was find somewhere quiet to rest.

"Marseille and then from there we can find a passage tae America. Ella…" He knelt before her. "I promise ye, things are going tae get better. We need tae leave our troubles behind now, make a new start… you, me and Ian. There'll be no more trouble, no McKenzies, no Red Coats, just a simple happy life in America, I promise you, hand on heart."

She managed a small smile for his sake, wondering if she had the strength to start again, but what choice did she have? Life had to go on and at least they had each other if nothing else.

The McKenzies were far enough away now, Ian could see Hamish up the other end of the dockyard, yelling at people to get out of his way, cursing that he had lost track of his prey. Ian made a quick dash as fast as he could, down the gangplank and along the dockyard in the direction of the ship that Ella and Fergus had boarded. But it was too late, he watched in horror as it drifted further away.

"No! Come back! No!" His cries were lost in the noise and the mayhem surrounding him, coupled with the shrieking gulls that were gathering over a fishing trawler coming into the harbour. The only thing he could do now was make his way to the mill and wait for Cousin Michael. It was too far to walk to Oaklands and he had no money to pay for a carriage. But more importantly, he needed to get away from the harbour and as soon as possible with the McKenzies looking for him.

Molly's eyes slowly opened, her knees were aching from kneeling on the hard wooden deck of the boat, she could still feel herself swaying with the rhythm of the sea. "I hope you're right," she said.

"I hope I'm right about what?" Ross sat down next to her under the tree.

She looked at him with confusion, then realised she was speaking to Ross and not Fergus.

"I... I..." She struggled to find her words.

"What happened, Molly, what did you see?"

"The McKenzies... they were after us... we boarded a ship to France." It was all so vivid in her mind and she could still feel the pain Ella carried in her heart.

"Where were we going?" Ross asked with intrigue.

"Marseille and then America, to start a new life."

"Well, that will explain why there was no further trace of Ella and Fergus in the history books or census for Aberdoch. Why did you come back tae the tree, I thought we were going tae leave all this behind you now?"

Molly stood up and brushed the leaves from her trousers. "I hope they found their happy ending," she said ruefully, without replying to his question.

"Well, we will have our happy ending, won't we?" Ross stood up and held her hand.

"I don't know. Will we?" she replied, sounding as glum as she looked. "Auntie is hell-bent on selling

Aberdoch Manor and…"

"Molly, she sent me to find you, she wants tae speak with you. I have a feeling it's about Aberdoch Manor, and I dinnae think it's bad news."

Molly turned to face him. "What makes you think that?

"She said it was important and I was tae come back with you because she wants tae speak with us both. If it was anything tae do with selling, she wouldnae need tae involve me, now would she?"

"To lay you off, maybe?"

"Well, she could do that without you present."

Daphne was still sitting in the armchair. The pain was less and the nap had done her good. It felt like all of a sudden, things seemed much clearer than they had done since her operation.

"Ah Molly and Ross, there you are. Sit down, both of you."

They sat without a word, both wondering why they had been summoned and both apprehensive about Daphne's news that awaited them.

"Having spoken to your mother," Daphne began, looking at Molly, "and having slept on the idea, I realise how important this place is to you… and to you too, Ross, with your ancestral connection, although why you want to hang onto the past is beyond me, but anyway, before I go any further, I need to ask you both something."

"What is it, Auntie?" Molly sat forward in earnest.

"Are you two serious about each other? I mean are you planning a future together, get married and so forth?"

Molly blushed. "Auntie, I don't think it's fair to speak about this now before Ross and I have really spoken about it ourselves."

Ross placed an arm around Molly. "I can't answer for Molly but Mrs Winters, yes I'm deadly serious about Molly and hope one day for us tae be wed and have a family of our own."

"You do?" Molly looked at him with relief and a smile.

"Of course. Don't you?" His voice wavered with concern that she didn't feel the same way, although her smile suggested otherwise.

"Yes, absolutely," she beamed.

"Well, that's settled then," Daphne said.

"What's settled?" Molly turned to her with a frown.

"Molly, I've decided to add your name now on the deed of Aberdoch Manor. I will be what they call a silent partner, so I believe. It means that you already own half of it and when I die, you'll own all of it. I want you and Ross to run it together, but obviously his name will go on the deed when you are married. I'll still stay living here for now but I think once the hotel starts making a profit, I'll look at moving into somewhere smaller, nearby. How does that sound? Can I trust you both?"

Their faces were awash with excitement. Molly rushed over to Daphne and kissed her on the cheek. "Auntie, thank you! Yes of course you can trust us!"

"Thank you, Mrs Winters!" Ross said, grinning widely. It was a big step up from being a gardener and he couldn't wait to run the hotel with Molly.

"What made you change your mind about selling, Auntie?"

"Your mum, mainly, she made me see how important this place is to you. So you can call her later, during cheap rate of course, and thank her."

"Oh, I will. I can't believe it!"

Chapter Twenty One

"Auntie, you look very nice," Molly complimented her. Daphne wore a navy blue dress with tiny white polka dots. She dusted her sleeves down with a clothes brush and looked proudly at Molly. "Well, I thought I should make the effort. You scrub up well, too. You should wear cornflower blue more often, it suits you. Oh, have you left all the bedroom doors open, so that people can wander in freely to inspect them?" She placed the clothes brush down on the coffee table. "And have you checked every single room and bathroom after the maids finished?"

"Yes, all is fine, stop worrying." Molly watched Daphne as she gave an attentive pat to the back of her hair, while glancing in the mirror above the fireplace for one last look of approval.

"I still don't understand why you asked that vicar to do the opening," she continued.

"Who else was I to ask? He is a strong pillar of the community, people round here look up to him, apart from you of course."

"You should have asked the mayor, the one from Eyemouth," Daphne said, ignoring Molly's dig at her not liking Norman.

"Well, I didn't," Molly replied indignantly. "And you should really put your grievances about Vicar Norman and Joan to one side, especially today. After all, they were the ones that organised the church fair and raised the money for treating the wood rot."

Daphne threw her hands up in surrender. "Alright! You don't have to go on about it. I told you before, I never asked them to help, you did. However, I'll make the effort for today as it is a special day."

"And you should thank him and Joan too," Molly added, knowing she was pushing her luck.

Daphne looked horrified. "Oh, now come on…"

"Aunt Daphne!" Molly frowned, flashing a warning look at her.

Daphne sighed. "Alright, if I find the right moment," she appeased her with no intention of doing so.

Ross walked into the living room. "People are arriving."

"Wow! You look very handsome in a suit," said Molly. "Very dashing!"

"And you look very pretty," he replied and then noticed Daphne's beady eyes on him, so he decided against kissing Molly on the lips in front of her, instead he gave a small peck on her cheek. "And you look very nice too, Mrs Winters," he smiled with a courteous nod of the head.

"Well, if we have finished dishing out compliments, we'd better go outside and greet the guests," Daphne said with a twinkle in her eyes. She watched Molly and Ross leave the room and sighed wistfully, pleased that she had changed her mind about selling Aberdoch Manor. It filled her heart with joy to see Molly so happy. Molly was the closest she would ever have to a daughter and suddenly she felt grateful; grateful to be alive, grateful to have her niece run the hotel, and also to be around young people and not stuck in some old people's home waiting for her number to be called.

"Wait, I have a surprise for ye first," Ross said, facing Molly.

"Oh, haven't you showed her yet?" Daphne asked

with surprise now standing at their side.

"No, I wanted tae wait until today."

"Show me what?" Molly looked at Daphne, perplexed and then back at Ross.

"You go on and show her, I can't walk quickly and I've seen it anyway."

"Seen what?" Molly asked again, baffled by their secrecy.

"Come on." He took her hand and led her down the hall, through the kitchen and outside around the back of the property. He stopped and walked behind her, covering her eyes with his palms. No peeking, so keep your eyes closed.

"But I might fall!"

"You'll no fall. Keep walking."

He finally came to a standstill and asked, "Are ye ready?"

"Yes!"

He removed his hands and she blinked hard against the blur. And then she saw it, a beautiful rock garden with sprays of dusty miller starting to bloom yellow surrounding a waterfall, and a plaque beneath that read *In Loving Memory Of Adam Buxton.*

"Ross!" She turned to face him with tears immediately springing to her eyes. "That's so beautiful. So very kind of you."

"Well, your aunt paid for it, but I made it."

"And was it your idea?"

"Yes," he admitted. "I thought if ye miss him, ye could come here. And over there…" He pointed to an area of grass near the stables. "I'll make one for Fergus too, so ye dinnae need tae keep going tae the Ghost Tree." He pulled her close. "I think we need tae leave the past behind us now. Do ye agree?"

"Yes I agree. Anyway, I have a feeling I won't need to

miss Fergus or Adam, not now that I have you."

"Well I am Fergus and Ross all rolled into one amazing gift!" he beamed. "Talking of gifts, I have one more for you." He pulled out a small, black box from the inside of his pocket and bent down. The cluster of three small diamonds, set into a band of white gold, caught the sun as he pushed the lid open. "Molly Hazleton, I feel like I have known and loved you forever, probably because I have," he grinned. "Will you do me the great honour of becoming my wife?" He waited with bated breath as she stared at him, then at the ring, with her hand covering her mouth. She knew one day they would get married but she had not considered he would propose so soon. Everything was happening really quickly - Adam's body finally found and laid to rest, Aunt Daphne deciding not to sell anymore, the big opening today. She was also trying to come to terms with the new knowledge of Fergus and Ella. That they had set sail to America to start a new life away from all the danger they were in. Would she ever find out what happened to them? Probably not, now she had just agreed with Ross not to go back to the Ghost Tree. There was so much to take in and her mind felt like a whirlwind.

"If it's not the right time, I will understand…" Ross said, sounding a little dejected by her long pause.

"No, it's the perfect time…" Her lips suddenly stretched into a beaming smile. "Ross, of course I'll marry you!"

There was quite a crowd gathering at Aberdoch Manor, a good turnout from the locals and many came down from the highlands and as far as Eyemouth, all curious to see the much talked about hotel that had been nothing more than a creepy run down old estate for many years. The chambermaids were handing out glasses of bubbly and

Mrs Brady had laid out an impressive array of hors d'oeuvres, showing off her culinary skills. Joan placed her infamous Victoria sandwich cake down on one of the tables, but Mrs Brady quickly whisked it out of the way. "I'll put it out later," she said, not wishing anyone else to steal the limelight.

A red bow was tied from either pillar at the bottom of the entrance steps.

Molly handed Norman a large pair of scissors. "Thank you, Molly."

Molly pulled Daphne closer. "Vicar Norman, Auntie has something she would like to say to you first." Molly raised her eyebrows at Daphne.

"Do I?" she replied, inwardly squirming.

"Yes, you do," Molly pressed.

Ross, after mingling with some of the guests, joined Molly and Daphne, intrigued at what was going on. It wasn't like Mrs Winters to be in the company of Vicar Norman.

"Well, um, it was good of you to organise the money for treating the wood rot, not that I asked you to, and quite frankly…"

"Auntie!" Molly scolded.

"I was going to say, quite frankly I'm touched by your generosity." She noticed Joan standing behind Norman, listening. "And you too," she said, looking at her, trying desperately to remember her name, but try as she might it wouldn't come.

Norman blinked hard several times. "Thank you, Mrs Winters, that means a lot to me, especially coming from you. It was mine and Joan's pleasure."

Daphne forced a smile. Joan, that was her name. She only ever thought or referred to her as *Mrs Fusspot*.

"But we can't take all the credit, it was everyone in Aberdoch who chipped in," Norman continued. "So perhaps you would like to make a speech after I've cut the ribbon?"

She stared back at him, aghast. "Oh… um… no… I'm not good at public speaking. I'll say thank you as I walk around if it's all the same."

Molly and Ross exchanged an amused look.

"Very well," Norman said, making his way to the steps. "Everyone gather around please. Ladies and Gentlemen," he said, bringing the scissors to the ribbon. "I am delighted to announce the opening of our very own superb hotel, putting Aberdoch on the map for tourists…"

"And weary hikers," Joan called out.

"Yes, there'll be many of those I daresay," he smiled. "And whoever else needs a comfortable and welcoming place to stay…"

Molly linked arms with Daphne, then raised her glass.

"Thank you to everyone and to Vicar Norman and Joan. Thank you for all your support and donations to fix the wood rot. And on behalf of myself, my aunt, and my fiancé…" She waved her ring finger in the air, then grabbed hold of Ross' hand, as everyone cheered at this sudden double celebration. "We couldn't have done it without you!

"Ladies and Gentlemen I give you Aberdoch Manor Hotel!" Norman announced at last.

"Aberdoch House of Horrors, it should be named!" Iris shouted out from the crowd.

Ross rushed over to her, grabbing her arm and pulling her to one side. "What is wrong with you? Why do you always have to make trouble?"

An evil grin appeared on her lips, enjoying the attention. "Because the McKenzies always have the last word, have ye no learned that by now, McDaniel?"

"To Aberdoch Manor Hotel!" the crowd echoed, raising a glass in the air.

Epilogue

The dew glistened over the lawns in the early morning sunshine. A woman and two children walked up the lane arriving at the grey stone archway. Aberdoch Manor stood tall and grand in the distance. The trio, weary and dishevelled, plodded on in silence.

Molly had been up since sunrise, checking everything for what seemed like the hundredth time in preparation for their first guests to arrive. Mrs Brady was cooking breakfast and the aroma of eggs and bacon wafted down the hallway, reminding Molly of her hunger and also her need for a strong cup of coffee. She checked the diary. Her index finger glided over the details of three guests booked into one room, the family suite. The name, *The Fergus McDaniel Suite*, didn't meet with Daphne's approval. She didn't see the point of using some old clan leader's name whom no one would have ever heard of, she would rather had named the suites after various local places of interest or her favourite flowers, but Molly had been insistent and so it was decided upon. Their first family were due to arrive this morning. Molly's eyebrows knitted together again. The surname seemed familiar but she couldn't quite place where or how she knew the name. Daphne had taken the phone call the day before and had written it in the book, saying the woman had a broad Scottish accent and it was difficult to make head nor tail of what she was saying. Perhaps Daphne had made a mistake with the name.

"Ah, there you are, have you had breakfast yet?" Daphne walked towards the reception with a spring in her step, now her hip was as good as new and not giving her any more pain.

Molly glanced up from the diary. "No, although I really should." Her stomach gave another impertinent rumble.

"Good, I'll join you," Daphne said.

"But what if someone arrives? We can't both go for breakfast at the same time."

"I can cover for you both," Ross said, walking down the stairs, having just changed a lightbulb on the landing.

Before Molly had a chance to reply, the front doorbell rang loudly throughout the property.

"We really should leave it on the latch during the day," grimaced Ross at the intrusive chiming that seemed to last longer than it should.

Daphne shook her head. "And let every Tom, Dick and Harry wander in?"

"How are the guests supposed to come and go if the door is always closed?" Ross sighed.

"Well, while you two argue it out, I'll let the guests in, shall I?" Molly rolled her eyes and left them to it.

"Fair point," Daphne replied to Ross. "I suppose as long as one of us is always around, it should be alright, although you best not rely on me as I will be leaving soon, once I find my perfect cottage."

"And we shall miss you greatly," he said, with a twinkle in his eye. "Mrs Winters, this is no Glasgow; we're in a remote hamlet in the middle of nowhere, it'll be perfectly safe tae leave the door on the latch."

The young woman was wearing a long dark skirt under a bright red cape that clashed a little with her auburn hair, scraped back neatly behind her head. The boy, looking to be around eleven years old and the girl a few years younger, clutching a ragdoll in her arms, shared the same colouring and pale complexion as their mother. All three of them stared back at Molly, wandering why she wore an expression of disbelief, bordering horror.

"Are we tae wait on the doorstep all day or are ye

going tae let us in?" The woman asked impatiently.

"Mrs…" Molly struggled to find her tongue.

"Mrs Barrack, aye. Mrs Shona Barrack and these are ma two children Ian and Lilly."

Molly froze, desperately trying to make sense of it all. Was she in some kind of weird dream? Had she travelled back in her mind without the Ghost Tree? How was it possible that Fergus' sister and children, who died over two hundred years ago, were right there, standing in Aberdoch Manor in the year 1946?

"Molly! For goodness sake!" Daphne muscled in, wondering what the hold-up was. "Please forgive my niece." She gave them the once over, then suddenly wondered if they had the money to pay for a room, that was probably why Molly was hesitant. They looked penniless. "You don't have any luggage?" She frowned at them.

"We lost everything in a fire," Shona replied. "But I have money, dinnae fash about that." She patted her pocket and flashed a fleeting, reassuring smile.

Daphne nodded, satisfied. "Please, do come in."

They passed Molly on the steps as she stood watching them, utterly speechless.

Time is relative and flexible, and the dividing line between past, present, and future is an illusion.
Albert Einstein.

About the Author

Claire Voet is an award winning, English author, born in Gosport across the shores of Portsmouth Harbour, on the south coast of England.

Claire started writing in 2010 and has since then written a number of books, including The Ghost Of Bluebell Cottage, The Other Daddy A World Away, Captain Hawkes, short story A Helping Hand, Echoes In The Mist, Outcast and now Outcast II - The Irish Connection.

Claire demonstrates her love for history and also the supernatural in many of her spellbinding stories.

www.clairevoet.com

Other books by Claire Voet

The Ghost of Bluebell Cottage
The Other Daddy A World Away
Captain Hawkes
Echoes in the Mist
Outcast

www.blossomspringpublishing.com

www.ingramcontent.com/pod-product-compliance
Lightning Source LLC
Chambersburg PA
CBHW031316170626
46807CB00002B/441